BETRAYED MATE

REJECTED FATE TRILOGY
BOOK 1

JEN L. GREY

CHAPTER ONE

My skin crawled.

I stood in front of the mirror that hung on the back of my closet door in my bedroom, taking in a reflection that didn't quite look like me—there was no flour on my shirt, and my hair wasn't pulled into a bun. Mating with Reid Blackwood felt right, but at the same time, nothing did.

The conflicting emotions bounced around inside me whenever I was near or thinking about him.

"Sis, you look beautiful," Briar murmured, tucking another red camellia into my hair. I looked as if I had a crown of flowers on my head.

I bit my bottom lip. My mouth had been painted red to match the color of the flowers, which helped my pale-green eyes stand out and complimented my copper-red hair as if this particular shade had been made for me. "Why are we putting a crown on my head? Father's made it clear he doesn't want to be king, and I have no intention of becoming queen myself."

Mom sighed and flipped her long blonde hair over one shoulder of her emerald-green dress. "Ember, many brides wear tiaras and crowns on their wedding day. There doesn't have to be additional meaning behind it. Even if you don't intend to eventually ascend the throne, this is an opportunity for the wolf packs nearby to join in a celebration of our family merging with the Blackwoods. We all need hope for the future after all the chaos we've suffered these past two months."

I rolled my eyes and looked into Mom's brown ones through the mirror. "Yes, because wolf shifters usually have wedding-like mating ceremonies." I let sarcasm drip from every word. The truth was that I didn't feel comfortable with any wolves outside of my pack in Shadowbrook, North Carolina. Apparently, that was one reason that Reid's and my fated-mate bond had taken so long to kick in—I'd stopped going to the regional wolf-shifter meetings with my father, so Reid and I hadn't seen each other in eight years. Not since I was seventeen years old. We probably would have already been mated for years by now if I had just attended the meetings, but I'd figured there was no point in putting myself through the discomfort; everyone had ruled me out as my pack's future alpha because I didn't have a dick.

Fate had a wicked sense of humor—the bitch.

"Honey, I know you hate being the center of attention, but this ceremony is a step toward unity again, even if it's only for a minute. It offers hope that our species can recover." She smiled sadly, the faint crow's-feet around her eyes becoming more pronounced. "Besides, you already agreed to it."

I had, but that was partly because I'd been caught off guard by the connection that sprang up between Reid and me when he and his dad, Perry—the Blackwood alpha—and a few other wolf shifters from their pack had come to check in on us about three weeks ago.

Two months ago, the entire royal family pack, the top-level alphas from each pack in the region, and almost the entire wolf pack whose job it had been to protect them had been slaughtered not even twenty-five miles away, and everyone was still on edge. Communications between packs had become harder since our regional alpha was no longer alive to coordinate news with every pack underneath him instantaneously through his pack links, and no new regional leader or royals had been chosen. We could link only with our own packs.

No one knew who'd attacked or why. It was like ghosts had killed them—well, all except for four from the protector wolf pack. They'd been called away just before the attack. Conveniently? Maybe.

Now, everyone suspected each other and was afraid they'd be next.

Briar brushed off her pale-blue dress and pushed her lighter copper hair out of her eyes. "That may be the hope, but we both know the Blackwoods have always had lofty goals. We all heard that Reid had been trying to date the princess." She winced and cleared her throat. "Fate bless her soul."

I snorted, sounding ever so much *not* like the princess everyone wanted me to be. Briar was so sweet compared to my bluntness. "I don't think you can offend the dead. Besides, you weren't talking poorly of her."

She narrowed her jade-green eyes at me and lifted her chin. "I wasn't worried about offending her—I just hate that they all died so horribly. Can you imagine the trauma they experienced in their last breaths?"

I inhaled sharply. Briar was only twenty-one, but she

sometimes seemed more mature than me despite my four years on her. "Fair point."

A knock came at the door, and I spun around, the edges of my cream dress flaring around my knees.

The door opened, and Dad stuck his head in the room. His dark-copper curls were wilder than usual, and shadowy circles sat heavy under his eyes. "Holy smokes." He chuckled, taking in the three of us. "I leave the house with three women in pajamas and drool at the corners of their mouths, and I return to find them all prim and proper. Had I known that this was what it would take—"

Mom waggled a finger at him and growled, "If you don't want to sleep in the wolf's den, you better stop right there." She pressed her lips together, but the corners of her mouth tilted upward.

Dad entered the room and sat on my full-size bed, his shoulders hunched. My maroon comforter hung halfway off the mattress where I'd thrown it this morning, and I winced.

Mom sat next to him and took his hand. "I thought you were going to get back in time to take a nap before the ceremony?"

I glanced out the window by the bed at the descending sun. It was almost time to leave for the cliff overlooking the dense forests that spanned the distance between our territories. Territories that might one day be merged under Reid's leadership if no one in our pack took over as alpha.

"With the mating ceremony upon us, both we and the Blackwoods are thoroughly scouting our territories to ensure nothing is remotely alarming." Dad squeezed her hand and kissed her cheek before continuing, "But I'll be fine. I'll drink some coffee and take a shower, and I'll be right as rain for the ceremony and the festivities after. At least two other packs have already shown up and are heading to the cliffs now."

My stomach clenched, and I wasn't sure if it was butterflies or something that indicated I needed to make a pit stop before we left.

"Well, you should move now." Mom smoothed out the wrinkles in her dress. "We need to head out too."

He laughed. "It's not like they'll start the ceremony without her."

My breath caught. I didn't like the sound of that...which was stupid. Of course they couldn't start without me. I was the female mate—er—bride... Hell, I didn't even know what to call myself. Not even the royals had mating ceremonies. Usually, the two fated or chosen mates performed the ritual and fully completed their bond by themselves. Instead, Reid and I were going to create a partial bond in front of all the local packs and then retreat to the house we'd be living in to complete it.

"Even so, we don't want to be late." Briar arched a brow. "What would that say about how we perceive this mate bond?"

Dad frowned. "You three win. But before I get ready, can I speak to Ember alone? There's something I need to—"

A howl came from outside the house. Craig.

My heart jolted, and I tugged on my pack link to him. *Are we under attack?*

No, Em. There's nothing for you to worry about. I just need to alert your dad to something.

My shoulders relaxed, and I took a deep breath. Even though there hadn't been another attack on wolf shifters since that night, something sinister seemed to be floating around all the shifters. Something we couldn't shake. It probably sounded crazy, but we couldn't rest until we determined who'd murdered our king and queen and everyone around them.

Dad sighed. "Craig's got something for me to take care of while I get ready, but Ember, I'd like to talk with you before you leave. There's something important I need to share." His green eyes narrowed uncharacteristically.

A lump formed in my throat. This was the fifth time he'd said that in the past week, and we were out of time. Every time he'd mentioned it, something had happened—with a scout or a lookout—or he'd received a phone call from another pack and needed to leave because they thought they'd sensed something off. However, he'd had that look—brows furrowed and the skin around his eyes tightened—only one other time... when he'd had to tell me that something was wrong with one of my cakes.

"We need to leave now, Atlas." Mom shook her head. "You'll have to tell her after the ceremony. I already made the coffee when you said you were heading back, so take a quick shower, and I'll pour you a cup. You can catch up with us."

Dad's jaw worked like he wasn't thrilled. "I won't shower—I'll just clean up a bit. Go on, I'll catch up shortly." He left my room, and my chest constricted. Somehow, I sensed whatever he had to say to me was way more important than I'd originally thought.

Looping her arm through mine, Briar tugged me toward the door. "Come on. It's four miles to the cliff, and the sun will be setting soon."

I grimaced but let her pull me along. What was wrong with me? I wanted to plant my feet on the shaggy brown carpet, but all that would accomplish was added tension between our packs, and right now, that would be the worst possible thing to happen.

Mom, Briar, and I stepped into the hallway. My gaze skimmed past pictures of our family in front of our house and white-water rafting and went to the room directly across from mine, Briar's. We wouldn't be able to hang out each night any longer. I glanced to the right and saw Dad disappear behind my parents' bedroom door, and a sense of loss sat heavy in my chest. Shouldn't starting a life with my fated mate make me feel more excited than this?

We left the house, the cool mid-October breeze brushing my face and blowing my hair back. The other brick homes of the pack neighborhood didn't have any lights on, indicating people were either already heading to my ceremony or guarding the territory.

My bare feet sank into the cool grass as we passed through the woods behind our house, following the trail to the cliff where Reid waited for me. The leaves of the oak and maple trees were turning from green to red, orange, and yellow, emphasizing that fall had arrived. This was my favorite time of the year—the views of the Blue Ridge Mountains were just plain gorgeous.

About a mile into the walk, I froze. Briar and my mom continued on a few steps before they realized that I wasn't beside them anymore.

Mom's brows creased. "What's wrong?"

"My dessert." I'd had no say over much of anything to do with the ceremony. Reid's mom, Mavis, had done most of the planning, wanting it to be perfect for her son, their pack's future alpha. The only thing I'd requested was that I get to make my signature dessert, which I'd done during my shift at the bakery where I worked early this morning. For any special event, I always made the same thing—red velvet cake with praline icing, topped with raspberries dipped in chocolate and maple syrup. It was a concoction I'd created when I was eight—I'd finally convinced Mom I was old enough to use her kitchen, and the dessert had been a huge family hit.

"Mavis picked it up this afternoon when you were taking a nap." Mom patted my shoulder. "She wanted to make sure that she got it in time for it to be incorporated into the buffet line. Reid stressed to her how important it was to you."

"Oh, okay." Some of the discomfort in my stomach eased. During the whole planning process, Reid had made sure my voice was heard, even when I hadn't wanted to make waves. This ceremony wasn't important to me; our relationship was. His mom could've planned the whole thing alone, but Reid was a good guy and had wanted me included.

So why did I feel so strange around him at times, like I couldn't wait to get away from him?

I shook my head and forced a smile, not wanting my mom and sister to worry about me. They had enough on their plates, and he was my fated mate. There was no reason for the two of us not to be together.

I blew out a breath and moved forward again.

Briar and Mom started talking about the ceremony and the night ahead. I smiled and nodded when they glanced at me, but I focused internally.

Without intending to, I eased in front of them. I was most definitely not in a hurry, but something had settled hard in my bones. The cliff was before us, and I could see about two hundred people standing in the trees, waiting for the ceremony.

My eyes were drawn to Reid. He stood near the cliff's edge, laughing and talking to a beautiful woman with dark tan skin who looked close to my age.

Cassiopeia, the witch who had grown up with the Blackwood pack, also stood at the cliff's edge, facing all of us, prepared to oversee the vows created for us to speak as a show of unity for our people.

Her golden-brown eyes focused on me, and she smiled.

A shiver ran down my spine.

I moved forward on autopilot and ran into someone's side. Warmth shot through my arm, and I jerked my head up to find a breathtakingly handsome man glaring at me. The first thing I noticed was the scar running through his left eyebrow. Instead of taking away from his handsomeness, it added an edge of sexiness.

Brown eyes with flecks of gold met mine, and he sneered.

Suddenly, Dad was on my other side, scowling at the man. "Ryker. What are you doing here?"

My head spun. *Ryker Grimstone.* The son of the alpha whose pack had been in charge of protecting the royals. One of the four who'd been mysteriously absent when the attack happened. I couldn't believe he had the nerve to show up here.

"I'm part of a local pack, and from what I heard, we were all invited." He rocked back on his feet, the wind ruffling the tips of his spiked hair. He smiled, but there was no warmth behind it. In fact, it sounded more like a dare, like he wanted to be asked to leave.

Dad, he wants you to make a scene. Let's just ignore him. I wanted to get very far away as quickly as I could. He might be the most handsome man I'd ever seen, but rumors swirled about him and everything he'd done. From what I gathered, he enjoyed pushing boundaries and challenging authority with his antics.

Taking my arm, Dad said, "Just stay away from my daughter. She's getting mated."

"Believe me. I don't want anything to do with her," Ryker shot back.

My throat tightened around a smart-ass retort. "The feeling is mutual," I spat before following Dad toward Reid.

Mom and Briar followed close behind us, but they didn't say anything, most likely because they were plastering smiles on their faces like me.

When we reached the front, Reid didn't acknowledge us. He just kept talking to the woman I'd never seen before.

I cleared my throat.

He scanned me with sparkling blue eyes, and his forehead creased.

"Everyone, it's time for the ceremony to start!" Cassi called, her long dark hair lifting in the breeze. "Reid, please escort Ember to me so you can begin the vows."

My fated mate adjusted the top button of his navy shirt and ran a hand through his shaggy, blond hair. Then he took my hand.

As soon as our skin touched, the tug indicative of the fated-mate bond yanked at me, but an equally strong but repulsive sensation had me wanting to pull away from him.

He sucked in a breath like he'd felt the same thing.

His eyes glowed, and he looked to my left. I followed his gaze to his parents, who stood a few feet away in front of the crowd. They had to be pack-linking to him.

Still holding my hand, he glanced at the strange woman one last time before guiding me toward the witch. With each step we took, Cassi's gray eyes grew warmer, and a smile spread across her red lips.

Behind Cassi, the forest of the Blue Ridge Mountains flowed away from the cliff. Sunset was upon us, casting golden light over both our territories. The timing of the ceremony was intended to emphasize hope and that we would survive.

"As you know, a mating ceremony isn't pack precedent, but any event that gives us something to celebrate and brings these two packs together in this trying time deserves to be special." Cassi clasped her hands in front of her chest. She stood so close to the cliff that the back hem of the black dress she wore drifted over the edge. "We're here to celebrate with the happy new couple before they merge their souls. What we will witness is their claiming of each other."

At least she wasn't pushing us to have sex in front of everyone. That should count for something.

"Please, Reid and Ember, turn toward each other."

The two of us obliged, and I looked up the five-inch height difference to stare into Reid's eyes. My gut twisted, and I wasn't sure if it was indigestion or butterflies.

"Reid, by biting Ember, you're claiming her as your mate for life and promising that you'll care for her as you would yourself. Will you make this vow and seal it with your bite?" Cassi gestured for Reid to bite my neck.

"I..." He coughed, his face flushing. He swallowed and sputtered, "Will."

My heart hammered as I moved my hair to one side, allowing him easy access to my neck and shoulder. He lowered his head, and his breath warmed my skin. I closed my eyes, waiting for the sting of piercing teeth, but nothing happened.

I opened my eyes.

Reid straightened. He shook his head. "I can't."

CHAPTER TWO

I blinked, trying to comprehend what I'd just heard. It couldn't be what I thought because this was our mating ceremony, and at least two hundred pack members were watching us.

Either I was having a nightmare, or I had completely misunderstood.

Taking a ragged breath, I reached for my hair and brushed it aside again, trying to ensure that I had moved it all, just in case that was the issue. "Is that better?"

Reid's forehead smoothed, and disgust twisted his features as he hurriedly took a step back. "No, that's *not* better."

"Reid." Cassi dropped her hands to her sides. "We're in the middle of the ceremony—you need to bite and claim her."

"I...I can't." He ran his hands through his hair. "I *won't.*"

My face flamed, but I refused to cower, not like this... not in front of so many people. For my pack and father, I wouldn't make myself look less worthy.

Murmurs rose from the woods where the onlookers stood, and Cassi glared at the woman Reid had been talking to when I arrived.

"Reid...you were the one who wanted this to happen." Cassi rolled her shoulders back and offered a strained smile and then spoke louder. "Don't worry, everyone! Just a little bit of cold feet. Who knew fated mates would have them too, before they completed their bond?" She laughed uncomfortably.

"It isn't cold feet." He crossed his arms, his biceps bulging against his shirt. "There's something wrong with her."

I took a step back, my foot hitting a rock that jutted from the ground. Pain burned up my leg and cleared my shock. "What are you talking about? We saw each other a couple of days ago, and everything was fine."

He lowered his clenched hands. "Well, there is something now. My wolf must sense something wrong with your blood. That's the only thing that makes sense!"

No one talks to my daughter that way, Father linked and snarled. He took a hurried step toward us, but Mom grabbed his hand and connected, *Don't. All the other packs are here. This is supposed to be a unity ceremony, not a cause for more of us to turn against one another.*

"Be reasonable, Reid," Cassi hissed under her breath, quiet enough that the others probably couldn't overhear. "You said she's your fated mate; you two have a bright future together. Your union makes the most sense in order to ascend the throne as the next king and queen and form a new royal pack."

Not the future I'd wanted.

I understood my father, my sister, and I were the last of the wolf shifters with a smidge of royal blood running through our veins, but the connection was from more than four hundred years ago when the youngest of four royal children had mated with my pack's then alpha. We weren't pure royal blood—there were three generations separating me and my royal ancestor. We weren't even considered royal...at least we hadn't been until two months ago when the slaughter happened.

In the aftermath, someone had pointed out that a royal had married into my family pack hundreds of years ago. Still, I'd had no thoughts about ever ruling. All I wanted was a quiet life with my pack and, eventually, my own bakery.

Cassi took my arm and tugged me closer to Reid, causing him to back away from us, his heels nearing the very edge of the cliff.

"I can't!" he shouted. "The longer I'm close to her, the more confident I am that something is *very* wrong with her. Don't you sense it? She's not fit to be anyone's mate—or even queen, for that matter."

Every cell in my body sizzled. I wanted to put my tail between my legs and run.

Was there something different, something off about me? Was that why our fated-mate pull didn't seem natural?

"What are you doing, son?" A spitting image of how Reid would appear when older, his father Perry, moved toward us from his spot in front of the trees. "You were howling at the moon over this last night—"

"Not anymore." Reid spat on the ground. "She repulses me. She's not going to be my mate."

Bile churned in my stomach. Not only was he rejecting me in front of hundreds of people, but he was calling into question my pack's legacy and standing within the community. Tears burned my eyes. I'd done the one thing I'd never wanted to do in my life—let down my pack and family.

Dad was our alpha, and he had two daughters. No sons. The best thing Briar and I could do was find a strong alpha mate to solidify our position because neither of us could take over our pack. And now I'd just done the complete opposite.

Shaking, I stayed in place, knowing I needed to leave but hoping that he'd laugh and proclaim his protest was some sort of cruel joke. Anything that wouldn't label my pack as strange or different.

Cassi released my arm, breaking my trance. I could still salvage this. Not wanting people to hear everything being said between us, I whispered, "Did I do something to upset—"

Reid jerked away from me and lost his balance, his foot slipping off the edge of the rock. He teetered on one foot, pinwheeling his arms.

Perry's eyes glowed as he jumped forward and grabbed his son's arm then yanked him forward. Reid fell to his knees in front of his father.

Perry turned to me and hissed, "Leave! Get out of here, and never come back."

His words were the ultimate slap in the face, and I stumbled away.

Strong arms clutched me, and a musky leather scent filled my nose, informing me who it was—Dad. *Come on, Em.* He tugged me gently toward the tree line where Briar and Mom waited. My vision clouded, and I tried to hold back the tears.

Falling apart would make this entire situation worse. I took a ragged breath and stared at the ground, not wanting to see the stares no doubt being cast my way. If only I could become invisible or evaporate.

When we reached them, Mom charged ahead while my sister took the spot on my other side. My family circled me, trying to protect me.

The night that was supposed to be a celebration of my special bond with my fated had instead become the worst situation any wolf shifter could face—I'd been made a fool of and disgraced. Everyone knew something was wrong with me.

The musky scents of wolf shifters assaulted my nose. Each whiff that hit my face made my stomach knot even more.

As we were about to break free of the attendees, a group burst out laughing. "Don't get too close to her; you might get loser vibes on you!" a woman who sounded like a teenager jeered.

Great, now people younger than me were calling me names.

Ignore them, Em, Briar linked with a growl. *They're idiots.*

If I'd witnessed what they just had, I'd probably be thinking similar thoughts, though I wouldn't have been as callous. I refused to kick others when they were down, but most shifters didn't think like my pack.

"It's easy to judge someone when you haven't been in their fur," a deep voice interjected, and the laughter stopped.

I recognized the voice, and a tear trailed down my cheek. This evening was growing worse by the second, and I was mortified that *he,* of all people, was standing up for me. Instead of making it better, Ryker Grimstone had put a larger target on my back.

The bastard.

"Of course the wolf who ran away while the royals and his own pack were slaughtered would side with *her*," a man hissed.

I walked quicker, and the scents of my own pack filled my nose. I blinked, clearing my eyes enough to see at least twenty of my pack members forming a barricade on either side of us, blocking the other packs from seeing me as easily.

Removing my arms from Dad's and Briar's, I wiped the moisture from my cheeks and lifted my chin. We'd passed nearly everyone, and I couldn't wait until I could run home without looking even weaker.

For now, I kept my pace steady, pretending I had some sort of dignity.

Dad and Briar must have sensed what I needed. They didn't attempt to hold me again. Instead, the three of us moved faster, and I exhaled as numbness overtook the shock.

At least I wasn't falling apart.

I focused on my breathing, trying to retain my internal calm. I needed to be strong for everyone.

The forty of us who'd come to the ceremony moved in unison, each person making a point to not look in my direction. I had no doubt that order had come from Dad.

In silence, we made it back to our neighborhood. I'd never been so relieved to see the clusters of two-story brick houses nestled on one hundred and fifty acres of the Shadowbrook Woods, which the nearest city was named for. Twenty-two of the twenty-five houses were occupied by our pack.

Our house was closest to the trail exit, and as soon as it came into view, the sting of pain and heat of anger began to pierce the numbness I wanted to cling to.

I picked up my pace, passing my family and beelining for the back door. As I rushed past the firepit, I shut down my pack link, wanting to be alone to process the hell of a night I'd just had. With my emotions surging back, I didn't want to risk talking to anyone.

"Ember!" Garret, one of my closest friends, called out to me.

Another tear slid down my cheek. I refused to turn around and let the pack members see me like this.

"Let her go," Dad rasped. "She needs some time alone."

Inside, I ran through the kitchen, my feet slipping on the cold tile floor and then down the hallway into my bedroom. I shut and locked the door.

Leaning my back against the painted white wood, I slid to the floor and let my heart crack open.

I wasn't sure how long I cried. All I knew was that my eyes were swollen, I couldn't breathe through my nose, and I had a pounding headache. I was quite certain that it stopped only because I'd run out of liquid to make more tears.

A hint of musky lavender hit my nose, so when a faint knock sounded on the door, I wasn't surprised at all.

"I know you're keeping your link inaccessible, but I wanted to let you know that I love you and I'm here for you when you need someone," Briar said softly from the other side of the wall.

My heart twisted painfully, stealing my breath. I sniffled. Shutting them out was selfish. They all cared about me and were worried.

I wiped my nose with the hem of my dress, stood up... and opened the door.

As soon as Briar saw my face, her own creased with worry. "Oh, sis." She placed her hands on my shoulders, but before she could hug me, I took a large step back, my eyes burning with unshed tears once more.

Clearly, I *hadn't* run out.

"Please, don't." I would prefer to link with her because each spoken word had me fighting a sob. But if I made my link accessible, I'd have a lot more people linking to check on me. I couldn't handle that. Not right now.

She dropped her hands and nodded. "No hugs. Got it. How about we get you out of those clothes?"

I glanced down at the cream dress Mom had bought me for this ceremony, and my heart tried to implode.

Turning toward my closet, I caught my reflection in the mirror—puffy, bloodshot eyes, the flowers in my crown hanging half off my head, and dirty feet. The only thing that didn't look bedraggled was the stupid dress. Reid had pointed it out in a catalog we'd been looking through after he'd declared that he wanted to celebrate our bonding with a ceremony.

Rage pounded in tune with the ache in my head, and I gripped the sweetheart neckline with my hands. Betrayal and agony egging me on, I ripped the dress in half and let it fall then marched to my closet. I picked out jean shorts and a maroon top and slid them over my body.

"Uh... I thought we'd get into pajamas and stream something together." She lifted a brow. "I heard there's a new season of *Nailed It*."

Yanking the camellias from my hair one by one, I shook my head. "Maybe later, but not right now. I have something else in mind."

Briar bit her bottom lip. "Em, if you're planning to go see Reid, I think it's best—"

"Fate, no!" I tossed each flower on top of my cream dress. "I don't want to see that asshole ever again." Tears began to gather once again, but I'd cried enough for one night. "What I have in mind doesn't require going to his territory."

"Can I come with you?" She rocked back on her heels.

I scanned her, taking in her jeans and black shirt. "Okay." In fact, it was probably best I didn't go alone. If one of the scouts from our pack saw me, they'd inform Dad, and I doubted my parents would leave me by myself.

Knowing it was inevitable, I opened my pack link. Where we were heading, we needed to be able to reach the packs in case of attack.

I grimaced, waiting for Garrett or his sister, Carol, to link, but my head remained silent.

"Dad told everyone to leave you alone tonight," Briar answered my unspoken question.

My shoulders sagged.

I scooped up the dress and wilting flowers and went to the kitchen, Briar right behind me. Our parents were in the living room, watching television, Dad in his leather recliner with his back toward the hallway and Mom sitting on the black leather couch.

At my footsteps, their heads snapped in my direction.

"Oh, Em—" Mom started.

"Please don't." Tears tried to escape again. "I don't want to talk about it. I just want to sit by the firepit with Briar. We won't be gone long."

Dad laughed, taking note of what I had in my arms. "That's fine. Do what you need to do, but don't stray from the backyard. It's too risky at night."

"Understood." I moved for the door then paused. "Oh, and Dad?"

He glanced over his shoulder once more. "Yeah?"

"Thanks for holding off the pack." I pressed my lips together, unsure if I was about to smile or cry.

"I'd do anything for you girls." He winked and smiled reassuringly. "And I know you need time."

Mom placed a hand over her heart like she did whenever she witnessed something that moved her, and I hurried out the door, not wanting to break down all over again. I had a mission, and it was simple.

Keeping on my heels, Briar stayed with me the entire way through the huge yard.

I went straight to the firepit and tossed the dress and flowers into the center. Then I snagged the long-stick matches we kept underneath the side, lit one, and tossed it on the pile.

"Uh... Are you sure you want to do this?" Briar asked. "I mean, what if Reid comes back and apologizes tomorrow? You'll—"

I snorted loudly, not trying to hold back my bitterness. My throat ached. "Fuck him. After what he did to me, there's no going back. Fated mate or not, I refuse to be insulted and tossed aside like that. He treated me worse than garbage."

During my crying bout, I'd come to one conclusion. I would never put myself in a position to be humiliated like that ever again. Our pack stayed away from the spotlight—it was our natural inclination—and the one time I'd gone against it, our entire pack and my family were shamed.

Tonight had proven one thing, I could trust only my family and pack. No one else. Maybe interacting with only them from now on would limit my options, but that was a risk I was okay taking.

The fire took over and devoured the flowers and dress.

As the orangish-red blaze grew taller, licking the air around it, it seemed to reflect my inner turmoil; my insides scraped raw and throbbing like the sensation of flames searing skin.

Briar remained silent. She knew me better than to try to get me to talk when I wasn't ready, just as I knew this scene was making her even more worried about me.

A chill ran down my spine, startling me, especially with the fire sparking in front of us.

This sensation wasn't from the cold.

Someone was watching us.

My gaze went tentatively to some thick brush at the tree line...and dark eyes met mine.

Eyes that seemed familiar but belonged to no one in our pack.

My breath caught, and I braced for an attack.

CHAPTER THREE

My heart sputtered and I blinked. As soon as I opened my own eyes again, the mystery eyes had disappeared like a figment of my imagination.

Had the flames made me see something that wasn't there?

Briar linked, *What's wrong?*

I inhaled deeply, but all I smelled was smoke and overtones of musk. With all the people traveling in for the ceremony, wolves that normally didn't enter our territory had needed to pass through it to reach the cliff, which was located on the property line that divided the Blackwood and Sinclair packs. Many had come in their animal form.

I thought I saw someone watching us. Knowing it was foolish to just stand here and hope the person would leave, I strolled to the brush and pulled it back. The space was empty, but the tantalizing scent of musky amber and pine hit my nose, overpowering the ash and tugging at the back of my mind.

My gaze darted to the woods, but I didn't see anyone

there. The scent had already begun to dissipate, indicating they'd left.

If they'd planned to attack us, there wouldn't be just one. Still, they could be scoping out the area in preparation for an assault. I linked to Dad, *The scouts need to keep an eye out close to the pack houses. Someone was watching us from the woods, and...* A lump formed in my throat, and I inhaled sharply, the identity of the person crashing into my core. *And I'm pretty sure it was Ryker Grimstone.*

After a pause, Dad responded by looping Briar into our link, *Both of you, get your asses in here now.*

The firepit— I started.

I'll handle it, Em. For the love of Fate, the two of you get in this house now, he reiterated just as the back door opened and he came outside. Dark copper fur was already sprouting all over his body, and his clothes began to rip as the shift overtook him.

His eyes glowed bright with his readiness to alpha-will us if we didn't move.

I grabbed Briar's arm and hurried toward the house. I wanted to scout the area with Dad, but if I tried to do it right now, Briar would demand to come along too. Though her wolf wasn't weak, she had a milder nature than Dad and I did.

Dad remained in place, watching the two of us. I knew he wouldn't move until we were inside, but howls informed me he'd already alerted the scouts and everyone else in the neighborhood.

As soon as the door shut, I heard Dad's paws hit the ground, quickly growing farther away as he headed into the woods.

Mom stood in the kitchen, eyes wide and chest heaving. "Are you two okay?"

Normally, I'd say something funny or sarcastic to try to cut the tension, but not today. That simple question shattered the anger that had fueled me, and my heart twisted painfully once again. The drastic change in emotions unsettled me—like I wasn't quite the same person.

Briar tugged me to her side as though she wanted to remind me that I wasn't alone. "We're fine. Em sensed Ryker, but I didn't notice a thing."

"I'm just thankful nothing happened." Mom shivered.

Trying to push the hurt away, I straightened. "The Grimstone pack is now only four people. It's not like they could do anything to our pack of a hundred and five." Our pack was strong despite what Reid had proclaimed.

"Don't underestimate them." Mom frowned. "They were the second strongest of us all. That's one of the reasons they guarded the entire royal pack. If Ryker and his friends had been there when the attack happened, and he'd survived, several packs would probably be in favor of him taking the crown, especially since he was so close to the princess. There were rumors they might have been fated mates."

I rolled my shoulders. "I should help with the search." I yawned, exhaustion catching up to me, and sagged against our round, dark maple kitchen table, which was near the door.

"You would've had a huge day even if the end weren't so..." Mom trailed off, looking up at the ceiling for answers. "Startling."

I laughed. That was a horrible word to use to describe what happened, but I appreciated her efforts. "Mom, let's call it what it truly was. A disaster. I just—" A sob lodged in my throat, and I swallowed it. I didn't want to break down again. I'd cried more tonight than I had in my entire life.

Fate had screwed me with Reid. I'd never let anyone have that much influence over me before, which made me feel worthless. Like something was wrong with me.

"Why don't you give it a minute for your dad and the scouts to finish?" Mom pressed her lips together. "And if all is well, then you take a shower and try to get some rest." She glanced at my feet.

I followed her gaze. They were caked in dirt, and I feared looking at my reflection in the mirror again. The woman I'd seen this afternoon and hadn't recognized was the complete opposite of me now. But the thought of taking a hot shower and soothing my swollen eyes and pounding head did sound like a dream. "Okay."

The two of them stared at me, making me feel as if I were under a microscope. My skin crawled like it had earlier. I sighed. "Well, let me go grab my stuff so as soon as the coast is clear, I can take a shower."

With that, I went back to my room. All my life, I'd tried to be strong. I was the firstborn of the pack alpha, and my two goals since I could remember were to make Dad proud and to one day own my own bakery. Both had always felt attainable, but not tonight. I'd already failed at the most important—making my father proud.

Nothing seems amiss, Dad linked with the entire pack. *If Grimstone was stalking the area, he must have been curious about us. I'll stay out with the scouts tonight, and we'll alert everyone immediately if anything odd happens.*

Just as quickly as the pack links had warmed, they went back to their normal temperature.

I linked with only Dad. *Do you need me to join the watch?* My throat tightened as I awaited his answer.

I'll take it tonight. You need your rest. You can help out tomorrow night instead. I don't want to let our guard down for several days. After what happened tonight, we need to stay on high alert in case someone does cause problems.

I could breathe once again. He wasn't treating me differently. I hadn't even realized that I'd been worried Reid's rejection would impact how he viewed me. I should've known better. *Okay, but if that changes—*

You'll be the first to know. I promise. You're still the strongest wolf in the pack after me.

At the validation, my eyes burned with tears once again. *I love you, Dad.*

I love you, too. And nothing will ever change that.

Wiping the moisture from my cheeks, I snagged a pair of maroon shorts and a black shirt from my closet and headed down the hall to the bathroom.

I stayed in the shower until the hot water ran lukewarm. Then I managed to drag myself out, change into my pajamas, and go to my room. A part of me worried that I wouldn't be able to fall asleep, but as soon as my head hit the pillow, I was out within seconds.

———

The next morning, I refused to hide in my room. Instead, I put on what—if she were still alive—my grams would've called my big-girl britches and showed up for work, even though I wasn't on the schedule. It worked out well because someone had called in sick, so I worked from five in the morning until five that evening when the bakery doors closed. I even tried to stay longer to help clean up, but my boss pushed me out the door, saying I'd been there long enough.

On my way home, I forced myself to look every pack member I came across in the eye. Each one had concern etched on their face, but I smiled and tried to pretend that everything was okay. That my world hadn't changed despite everything inside me feeling strange.

Last night, I'd dreamed of the way my connection to Reid had seemed to both provide comfort and unnerve me. That would've been fixed if we'd completed our bond.

These repeated intrusive thoughts wouldn't accomplish anything but to drive me crazy. A fated mate hadn't been meant for me.

At home, I crashed for several hours.

My alarm buzzed, startling me from yet another dream of Reid, though this one was different. In this version, Reid didn't reject me, but right before we would have completed the bond, he morphed into Ryker as he bent down to claim me. Waking up, my whole body felt disappointed, and the sensation of having my heart ripped out debilitated me.

I sat up in bed, gripping my white shirt over my heart as if that would keep the organ from imploding in misery. Tears clouded my eyes, but I blinked them back. I had a task to do, and I needed my senses to be on high alert.

Shoving off the maroon sheets, I stood and stretched, needing to feel the burn in my muscles. I rolled my shoulders back, getting limber so shifting would be easier.

Someone knocked on my door, and Briar linked, *I heard your alarm, so I'm assuming it's time for us to join Garret, Carol, and the other scouts.*

I opened the door and lifted a brow. *You're joining the night watch?* I suspected that she and Dad wanted her there to support me, but I wouldn't call them on it. If Garret or Carol asked too many questions, she'd be there to help me fend them off.

She smiled and tilted her head. "I thought we both

were, but maybe I have a mouse in my pocket since you don't seem to be part of the equation."

I rolled my eyes but smirked, once again missing Grams. She'd used so many Appalachian sayings most people had never heard before, and she'd know exactly what to say to me right now to get my head back in order. "You're mouse-free. I am, in fact, part of the watch tonight."

Briar winked, knowing she'd pulled the right heart-strings.

"Come on, let's go." I threw an arm around her shoulders, and the two of us headed to the living room. Dad was passed out on the recliner, snoring, and Mom had in earbuds, watching a show on her phone.

Still, given her wolf hearing, she looked up as soon as we entered.

You two be safe. She pursed her lips. *And I'll have a huge breakfast made for you in the morning when you get back.*

The thought of food made my stomach revolt, but I didn't want to hurt her feelings. *Sounds great.*

I hurried over and kissed her cheek, and then Briar and I went out the front door. The cool breeze hit my face, and I glanced up at the full moon. My wolf stirred inside me.

She'd been quiet so far, as if the trauma had impacted her just as hard, but now she came surging forward within me. I stripped off my clothes and allowed her to take hold as Briar did the same.

My bones broke, and my skin tingled as fur sprouted. Within seconds, I was on all fours in wolf form with more enhanced vision, hearing, and sense of smell than I had in human form.

Briar stepped beside me in animal form, and the two of us waited for orders.

I yanked on my links to the twenty other wolves who were running watch tonight. *What area do you need us to cover?*

Fred, my dad's official beta, replied, *Do you mind taking the route behind your house?*

His words were the equivalent of a punch in the gut for so many reasons, but that assignment meant that they weren't thinking about Reid and me. *Sure—*

Wait. I meant the area directly across *from your section of woods,* he corrected hurriedly.

There it was. He'd realized his error.

I refused to let them all know how much last night bothered me, so I fudged the truth. *It's fine. Briar and I are already in the woods by our house.*

Briar shook her head and whined. *Damn, Em. Did you have to lie? I wasn't ready for the smell of rotten eggs.*

Of course she'd smelled my lie. *I don't want them to think I can't handle it.* I bounded in the direction of the trail we'd taken a little over twenty-four hours ago.

Briar fell into a slow run beside me.

Are you sure? Garret linked to me individually. *No one would blame you if you'd rather not be anywhere close to the Blackwoods.*

Garret was Fred's son and a year older than me. He spent a lot of time at our place with his father, so we'd become friends at a young age. *I'm fine. Promise. I just want everyone to forget the whole thing.*

After an extended pause, Fred linked back with everyone, *Okay, Briar and Ember will cover the route toward the Blackwoods' territory.*

Ahh... Garret and Fred had been checking in on me. That was fine. I'd gotten my way.

If you need me, just link, and I'll be there. Carol is

breathing heavily over here anyway and driving me crazy, Garret teased.

I laughed. His little sister was two years younger than I was, landing right between Briar and me in age.

Deciding not to encourage him with a response, I focused on the sounds of the woods. Raccoons scurried by, and owls hooted. Some distance away, it sounded as if a fox or smaller predator was hunting for food. Nothing seemed out of the ordinary.

The world hadn't changed yesterday. The only things impacted were my trust and heart.

Briar and I scouted nearly to the property line and had just turned around to head back when my hackles rose.

I glanced over my tail, but there was no sign of anyone behind me.

What the hell? *Briar, do you sense anything, or is it just me?*

I...I thought I was imagining things. I don't see or smell anything around us.

A yelp sounded close by, and my blood turned to ice.

The pack link to one of the scouts who'd been running the stretch beside ours grew cold, indicating he'd died.

I was instinctively lifting my head to howl in mourning when Fred linked with us all, *Everyone. Get ready to fight.*

CHAPTER FOUR

I didn't need an alpha connection like Dad had in order to know our pack was terrified. My heart pounded against my rib cage, and adrenaline had my wolf senses even more on edge.

Dad responded as my legs pushed me closer to our home. *What happened to John?*

Despite knowing he'd just woken to the kind of nightmare no alpha wanted, he sounded fully aware; the burden of the pack's health fell heavy on his shoulders. A burden I didn't even want to imagine.

I don't know. He linked, saying he needed help, but then he died before he could explain. Fred paused, most likely to collect his thoughts, and it felt like hours rather than mere seconds before he continued. *He wasn't able to indicate who attacked him.*

A whimper came from my side, and I turned and saw fear in Briar's eyes through the faint glow of magic from the pack link.

My stomach knotted. I wanted to tell her everything would be okay, but I couldn't make that promise. If the

Grimstone pack hadn't been able to fight off these attackers, I feared we wouldn't be able to either. Then again, our pack had about the same amount of strength, but none of our strongest fighters would run off. We'd fight and die together.

I'm— Carol connected but never finished as her pack link cooled.

We need help. Now! Garret sounded close to hysterical.

My tongue lolled out of my mouth as I picked up my pace. Still, I couldn't run too fast and leave my sister behind as I was certain we were being watched. Terror clutched inside my chest at the thought of her getting hurt or worse.

Where are you? Dad linked, his words slow and steady, exuding calm. However, I knew the truth. He was a bundle of nerves but was pushing through them to be the alpha everyone here deserved.

Instead of a verbal response, Garret's pack link turned cold.

A sob choked me, but I held it back. I couldn't lose focus. I had to protect Briar if it came to that.

What do we do? Briar panted hard next to me.

She was struggling to keep pace, and I couldn't push her harder. But then the sound of paws from the direction of the Blackwood pack hit my ears.

Do you hear that? Briar glanced behind her toward the Blackwood territory and slowed down a smidge.

A smidge we couldn't afford right now. *Yes, I hear it, which means we need to get back to the others now. We can't let them surround us and close in on us before we can reach the rest of the pack. We can't risk slowing down.* Were the Blackwoods attacking us? I linked with the others, informing them of my suspicions.

Briar focused forward and quickened her pace.

Good. Let adrenaline push her.

Making sure not to leave her behind, I listened to the sounds of the woods as we dashed by. There seemed to be no wildlife in the area, making my insides coil. Clearly, they'd sensed a predator, same as us.

The trees blurred as we pushed our animal forms to the fullest extent possible.

Another yelp cut off into a gurgle, and another pack member link disappeared. My heart fractured. Between losing four pack members and my future with Reid in a thirty-six-hour window, I'd had the security of my world stripped from me. All because of the fucking bond I had—er —had had—with Reid.

Dad connected with Briar and me. *Girls, I need you to run to the Asher pack for help. Everyone is now in wolf form, and the attackers are closing in on us. You're on the outskirts, so I need you two to peel off and get them.*

My wolf wanted to growl, but I didn't want to alert anyone who might not be aware of us to our location. *You want us to leave when our pack needs protection?*

For Fate's sake, Ember. It's not like that. You're running to get help and bringing them back with you. Not running away from a made-up threat.

Fair point. Leaving went against our nature, but if Dad wanted us to ask for help, we were in worse shape than I wanted to grasp.

Of course we'll go, Briar cut in.

Can't we call them? I pushed, not wanting to leave my pack behind even if it was for a worthy cause. Besides, I suspected there could be ulterior motives. *If we need help, then Briar and I—*

Dad interjected, *I can't afford anyone to shift right now. They're on us. Dammit, I need you to hurry.* Alpha will pulsed through the bond, and my knees weakened slightly, though I continued to push forward. *Go to the Ashers and get help. Bring them back so we can survive.*

Fine, but I'm not happy about this.

I angled around our neighborhood, trying to account for how the Blackwoods would close in on our pack. I raced in front of Briar, the sound of her paws digging into the mulch right on my tail.

I let anger numb my agony and push me forward. It was at least ten miles to the Asher pack. My chest squeezed with consternation, but I believed in my pack. We were strong, and we should be able to face down an adversary. Dad had to know that. Otherwise, why have Briar and I run to a neighboring pack and risk looking like deserters, like Ryker and his friends?

The yelps and clamor of battle grew louder as we closed in on the houses. We'd see the neighborhood as we crossed the road that led into our community and headed through Shadowbrook and beyond to the Asher pack's territory.

Several wolves howled a warning, adding to the unusually creepy vibe of the full moon. Normally, these were the best nights for runs, but tonight was filled with death and horror.

I wanted to respond. Packs were meant to mourn together, and all of us were heartbroken after the losses we'd suffered, and we needed to express our pain in the only way we knew how.

Briar was panting louder than I'd like, but we didn't have the luxury of taking it easy, and I refused to leave her alone out here. At least if something did happen, we'd have each other.

The neighborhood came into view just as three more pack members' links went out within seconds of each other.

Unable to deny the pull, I glanced in their direction, and my stomach soured.

Reid's familiar blue eyes glowed as he lunged toward Rosa, one of my female pack members. Rosa jerked back, whimpering.

Before I could see the impact, something slammed into my side, and I fell over.

Ember! Briar linked.

My side raked against the concrete and started throbbing. I jumped back to my feet. *Run, Briar. Go on; I'll be right behind you.* We never ran all out in front of other packs due to the unique speed of movement my family had and others didn't, but now wasn't the time to worry about exposing that unique strength.

A Blackwood wolf snarled and charged toward me.

No. I didn't have time for this.

Something sharp pierced my side, and I swiped my back claws. A strangled whimper came out, and the thick musk of my attacker hit my nose.

I took off, racing toward my sister. I had to catch up to Briar before she got attacked.

The sound of someone chasing me pushed me to go faster. The breeze picked up, blowing the wind through my fur. I ignored the throbbing in my side and didn't waste time glancing back.

I reached her where the terrain dipped, heading downward toward the river. If we could reach the river and submerge, we should be able to float downstream and hide our scents from anyone trying to track us.

I linked, *If you can run faster, do it. We need to make it to the water. Someone is chasing me.*

I'll try to match your pace, she replied, though I could see the fatigue already hitting her.

I couldn't believe that Reid insulting and rejecting me hadn't been enough last night. Now he and his pack wanted to slaughter my family? Had they been behind the attack on the royals too? But that didn't make any sense. They weren't as strong as the Grimstone pack... Unless they'd been working with Ryker? He had shown up to our ceremony.

When Reid and I had learned of our fated connection, he'd thought we could become the next rulers due to my blood. Maybe now he wanted to eliminate my possible claim to the throne?

I had never taken him for that type of guy.

Even more pack links dimmed within me, and my breath turned ragged. All these deaths were my fault.

My front paw snagged on a tree root, and I nearly fell. *Focus, Ember*. None of that mattered now. I could figure it out later—after we got help.

The river gushed ahead of us, indicating a strong current and muffled some of the sounds of our attacker, making them sound farther away. However, I knew better than to lower my guard.

My paws hit smooth rocks, and the water came into view. The river was flowing rougher than normal from all the rain earlier in the week. We were in the homestretch.

Somewhere behind us, a branch cracked, and Briar whimpered. Paws skittered and slid on the rocks, and her body crashed into mine—hard. We tumbled down the embankment, the rocks cutting into our skin and the steep drop stopping us from getting our paws underneath us. Briar hit her head on a rock...and then we dropped.

I took a large breath and crashed into the cold water. My instincts kicked in, and I started dog-paddling. The current washed me downstream quickly and made staying above the water a struggle. Frantically, I searched for Briar, and when I found her, I nearly stopped breathing.

She'd sunk under the water, eyes closed and pack link cool. *No.* We hadn't come this far for her to drown. I refused to lose anyone else I cared about.

I tugged my wolf back. It would be way easier to save Briar in human form. My wolf tried to fight me, not wanting to retreat when I needed her most, but I yelled the words *pack mate* in my mind.

She begrudgingly withdrew, and I shifted back into human form. My wounds ached and throbbed as my skin stretched and changed, but I worked through it, using my arms and legs, even as they changed, to swim closer to Briar.

I dove under the surface, my lungs already screaming for oxygen. If I risked taking a breath before retrieving her, then she could pass by me, and I might never find her again. My hand touched wet fur, and I wrapped one arm around her wolfish body and kicked with all the strength I had left to get to the surface.

Even more pack links extinguished. My chest panged for more than just air. Our pack was being ripped apart, and now Briar was injured.

The edges of my vision turned black as unconsciousness threatened. I gritted my teeth, ignoring my burning muscles and supported her added weight. Even as I moved forward, more spots cooled off.

Almost half our pack was gone.

We broke the surface, and I gasped just as water splashed into my face and down my throat, causing me to choke. What the hell had I done to Fate to piss her off this much? No matter where I turned, things got worse instead of better.

I searched for something—anything—to grab onto as

darkness continued to curtain my vision. *There.* My gaze landed on a huge limb to the left of us. I swam, coughing and choking, dragging Briar with me. My arms grew weak, but I held her fast.

Strength nearly gone, I reached the log and hoisted Briar onto it. Her head flopped against the side of the sizable branch, but her chest moved up and down as water trickled out of her mouth.

Thank Fate, she was still alive.

The edge of the log caught on something, and my light hold slipped. I dropped back into the water and thrashed, barely managing to keep my head raised. I reached out, desperate for something to cling to, but came up with nothing.

Something hit my back. I turned, hoisted myself on it... and my vision went black.

———

Wetness hit my face.

My eyes fluttered open. The world was dim, like it wasn't quite day or night, and a tall presence loomed over me.

My body felt sluggish, like I'd just fallen asleep. This had to be a dream.

"You need to wake up," a raspy, sexy voice muttered. "I don't understand why you'd do something so reckless."

I identified that voice instantaneously, despite having heard it only once.

I forced my eyes wide open, expecting to be in my bed in my room. Then everything crashed over me.

My chest wasn't cold because I was out of range of the pack. They'd all died...including my parents.

My breaths turned erratic until the faint pulse of Briar's link centered me.

She was alive but asleep or unconscious. I had to find her and get away from the person standing over me and speaking with such disdain. A person who could kill me at any second.

Ryker Grimstone.

CHAPTER FIVE

I tried clenching my hands, but it took a moment for my body to respond to the command. My muscles burned and ached like I'd worked out harder than ever before. How the hell was I supposed to fight him when I couldn't even make a solid fist?

"Is your pack searching for you?" Ryker's nose wrinkled, and he spoke slowly, like I might not understand.

The question had my heart sinking. No one was searching for me...including Briar. If I didn't locate her soon, I might not have any family or pack left. However, even crying seemed to require too much energy right now.

Ryker ran a hand through his hair, disheveling it. "Don't tell me that your pack kicked you out after what the entitled douchebag did to you the other night. I find that hard to believe, given how the alpha and the other pack members shielded you."

Reid.

He'd rejected me and embarrassed me, and he'd been there when my pack was killed, though I hadn't seen him murder anyone personally. If Dad hadn't alpha-willed Briar and me to get help... I stopped, unable to continue that train of thought, but betrayal and loss swelled inside me.

Tears streamed down my cheeks, and I tried to sit up. Mud squished between my butt cheeks and clung to my back.

Fuck.

I was naked. I'd shifted to save Briar, and I didn't have any clothes with me.

I splatted back into the mud, unable to stand, and cried even harder. I'd fallen so far in so many different ways. Near packless, weak, rejected, and now completely naked in front of Ryker Grimstone. I was about as low as I could go.

Ryker, possibly the biggest traitor ever to the wolf-shifter population, stared at me.

"Fuck," he gritted out, reaching for one of my hands.

He gripped it tightly, helping me upright. I moved slower than a sloth.

The world spun around me, and the mud filled even more crevices, uncomfortable and cold. He released me, and I wobbled to and fro like the damn kids' nursery rhyme.

He sighed loudly. "You're worse off than I thought."

Even though my heart remained steady, I understood the threat underneath those words. If he found me annoying, he'd kill me, and no one would ever know who'd done it or why.

I didn't want to die. My sister was out there, and I had to find her. I swung my arm, aiming for his face but hitting air. My body tilted toward the ground.

Ryker growled and wrapped an arm around my waist, his skin's warmth searing me. He hoisted me up and dragged me several feet back, my heels leaving trails in the mud.

"If you're gonna kill me—" I started.

"If you keep this up, I *might*," he spat. Sharp edges of thick bark pressed into my back and helped aid my balance as I sat against a tree. "I should've known helping another wolf shifter would be more of a pain in my ass than it was worth." He turned away and stalked to the gushing river.

I breathed in, smelling air thick with moisture. Drops of rain hit the ground and my legs. Of course it was raining. That sounded about right with my luck.

A shiver racked my body, and a coldness I'd never experienced before crept into my bones. If not for the faint warmth of my sister's pack link connection in my chest, I'd be physically and emotionally numb.

A part of me wanted to call out to Ryker. I didn't want to be alone—especially naked and alone—but I kept my mouth shut. He had made it clear he'd have no problem killing me, and I could manage on my own. I needed to get my bearings, and then I'd figure out *something*.

He trudged away from the river. I expected some sort of emotion to hit me, even if it was sadness, but I remained propped against the tree, blinking, waiting for *nothing* to happen.

Swallowing, I prepared myself to stand once again. I leaned forward, readying to get my feet underneath me, but the world spun faster. Nausea roiled in my stomach, and I begrudgingly leaned back against the trunk. I needed to eat and sleep before I could do anything to defend or protect myself.

I scanned the area for berries, but my eyelids grew heavy. Each time I blinked, my eyes were harder to open... until I couldn't. Against my brain's protests, I passed out.

My body shook like I was experiencing an earthquake.

"Wake up," Ryker said gruffly. "You need to eat and drink something so you can get your strength back." He shook me again.

My eyes popped open, and bile inched up my throat. "Stop," I muttered. "Going to throw up." I swallowed, hoping to maintain some remnant of dignity.

He jerked his hand back like he'd been electrocuted. My body stilled, and my stomach eased a little.

After a long moment, he exhaled. "You good now?"

Good was a stretch, but I wasn't up for talking. "A little."

He held out a bottle of water and a couple of sticks of jerky. The scent of dried, salted meat made my stomach rumble, and that's when it hit me. I hadn't eaten since before the mating ceremony. The lack of calories had caught up to me.

I snatched the meat and water from him and took a large bite. The food tasted like heaven, but I struggled to swallow it past my dried, parched throat.

With shaky hands, I unscrewed the bottle of water and took a large sip, dislodging the stuck meat. I coughed and took a deep breath.

"Okay, you seem to be getting better." He rubbed his hands together and stepped back. His gaze drifted below my face.

I felt too awful to care, though I suspected, when I looked back on this moment, I'd be mortified.

Instead of answering him, I focused on the things that would most definitely keep me alive—food and water. Ryker was more of a threat than an ally, though the thought of what I should do next petrified me.

Reid would figure out, if he hadn't already, that Briar

and I weren't killed along with the rest of our pack. He knew where I worked, so I couldn't go back there. Once I found Briar, we'd need to restart from scratch, with no money, while trying to replace everything, including essentials like clothes and food. We could live in the woods for a while in animal form, but that wasn't helpful when it came to making money, and wolf shifters weren't meant to stay in either form too long.

If I could get to my feet, I could shift into wolf form and hunt. I needed to be strong enough that Reid couldn't easily find me and finish me off.

My eyes burned, and I blinked and swallowed. I didn't want to cry in front of Ryker.

Multiple pairs of footsteps hurried in our direction.

"I'm heading out." Ryker gave me a semi-salute then spun around and headed in the direction of the footsteps.

I shoved the rest of the stick of meat into my mouth and chewed, hoping the energy would hit my system fast.

The world did steady around me as I took a large gulp of water. I tried to stand, but my feet slipped, and I landed back on my ass yet again, introducing mud into even more precarious places.

"Ry, what the fuck are you doing?" a raspy voice asked. "You took my breakfast and ignored me this morning. We thought something was wrong."

"I didn't ignore you." Ryker sounded annoyed. "I told you I was handling something."

"Something...or some*one*?" a third man asked. "Because you're definitely hiding another wolf shifter."

"Bruh, no," a fourth voice interjected. "Tell me you aren't torturing someone else? We talked about this. We're going to get a worse rep."

My heartbeat quickened. The food and water were

helping me. But then a lump formed in my throat. What if he'd drugged me and it hadn't taken effect? But why would he do that? He'd given me some of his food.

I didn't have a clear head.

"I'm not torturing anyone." Ryker's tone held an edge of warning. "We should head back."

"Man, what don't you want us to see?" The footsteps came closer, and I got onto my hands and knees to crawl away. My front side didn't have as much mud on it, so I moved to the other side of the tree and rubbed mud all over it as well. It would reduce my scent and at least put a barrier between me and them, albeit a small one.

The three new people got close, and I cringed. There was no way I wouldn't get caught.

Their musky scents floated in my direction, and I grabbed a medium-sized rock and placed it behind my back. If they decided to harm me, at least I had something to catch them by surprise. A split second could make a difference—me being alive right now was proof of that.

A man walked past the tree and froze. His head turned back, and he scanned me.

My breath caught, and I didn't move. I didn't have even a quarter of my strength back and couldn't shift.

"Uh... What do we have here?" It was the man with the raspy voice scratching his head. He had tan and dark brown hair, which stuck up messily. His brows furrowed. The skin around his dark eyes tightened.

I hated being talked about as if I wasn't a person, but I bit my tongue. I was outnumbered.

"Wait." Someone hurried over. "Don't tell me that Ryker has been keeping a *female* from us." A new man with fair skin appeared on the other side of the tree trunk, his navy-blue eyes widening as he took in my state. He jerked his head back, his sleek, dirty-blond hair hitting his face. "Uh...what the hell? It's cold out here. What do you think you're doing, Ryker?"

Yeah, I could only imagine how I appeared to them. In fact, not knowing had to be for the best.

The blond, fair-skinned guy removed his black shirt from his body and bent down in front of me.

I flinched, unsure of his intent, but then he held it out to me. "Here, take it. You've got to be freezing."

Even though the shirt wasn't thick, it would cover me. I didn't hesitate to slip it over my body. Mud clung to the fabric, but the material alone left me not quite as vulnerable. "Thanks," I croaked and cleared my throat.

"Gage, she'll be fine." Ryker sighed from the other side of the tree. "That's why I brought food and water. She was already doing better. We need to head into town."

A third person appeared behind the blond, fair-skinned guy, a scowl on his dark-skinned brow. He closed his milk-chocolate-brown eyes in what had to be disgust. He ran a hand through his dark locks, pulling them away from his face. "Are you okay? Did Ryker do this to you?"

"Really, guys?" Ryker scoffed, appearing on the other side of the man with tan skin. "You think I would do that?"

"I don't know." The fair-skinned guy shrugged. "You've done some shit I never thought possible."

"Fuck you, Gage," Ryker spat.

The dark-skinned man with locs squatted beside me. His eyes were kind, and some of the tension I'd been carrying floated away. He touched my shoulder, making sure to keep his hand only on the shirt. "What happened to you? You're a wolf shifter—why are you out here without a pack?"

His gentle words cracked a dam I hadn't even realized I

had. The numbness disappeared, and tears streamed down my face once more. I tried blinking to hold them back, but it only made them come faster and harder.

"Hey, it's okay. You're safe here." He squeezed gently. "We won't let anything happen to you."

The irony of the Grimstone pack proclaiming they would protect me wasn't lost on me. The last people they'd vowed to protect had been slaughtered. Still, this was a kindness I'd never expected to receive after what Reid had done to me, and that counted for something.

"Kendric, come on. Don't make her promises we can't keep." Ryker glanced from me to Gage's shirtless body and wrinkled his nose. "Guys, we don't have time to protect someone else. We need to stay focused on finding out who killed the royal family and our pack."

The tan-skinned man shook his head. "I don't know what happened to you, but you're not even close to the Ryker you were two months ago. We can't leave her like this. Clearly she's gone through something traumatic."

Learning the four of them were at odds was surprising, especially since alpha power emanated from Ryker.

"I'm with Xander and Kendric." Gage waved a hand in front of me. "We can't just leave her like this."

Enough talking about me like I wasn't here.

"*She* will be fine." I pointed to myself. I wiped the tears away, streaking the mud on my hands. Lovely. I must look like a complete train wreck, but that was the least of my problems. "I need to be on my way." I'd have to use my pack link to track down Briar, which would probably take a while. I doubted she'd return home. "Besides, I have to locate my sister."

Wanting to get away from the four of them and all the attention, I braced one arm against the tree trunk and hid my other hand, which clutched the rock I'd kept behind my back, as I stood. My knees threatened to give out, but I managed to stand.

"Your sister?" Gage smiled. "Tell me more."

Xander reached over and punched him in the arm. "Don't start your shit right now. It's not the time."

"What happened to her?" Kendric didn't acknowledge the other two.

That was an excellent question. "I...I don't know. She hit her head on a rock and fell into the river, so I shifted back to human form to help her. She was unconscious, and we were floating down the river together. I managed to push her onto a big branch, but then I came close to drowning. I woke up on the side of the embankment here with Ryker standing over me."

Terror and pain gripped my heart until I thought it would splinter. The agony was so intense that I wasn't sure I could go on, but I didn't have a choice.

"We can help you find your sister." Kendric pressed his lips together. "I take it she's not close enough to pack-link?"

I shook my head. "She feels faint, but she's alive."

Ryker grumbled. "I pulled her from the river, and now she's fine. We don't need to do anything else. Besides, even if we help her find her sister, it won't change their situation." Ryker lifted a brow my way. "Tell them you were forced to leave your pack."

Gage tilted her head. "Why would they kick her out?"

Ryker chuckled darkly. "Because she was the one that prick alpha rejected."

Rage slammed through my body. "My pack *didn't* kick me out. Briar and I were running for help when we were herded into the river."

"What do you mean, help?" Ryker's demeanor changed,

and he focused on me like I was suddenly the center of his world.

"My pack..." I needed to say it out loud. "They were murdered. Briar and I are the only two who got away."

Ryker's eyes glowed, and he leaned into my space.

I winced and adjusted my grip on the rock.

CHAPTER SIX

Ryker's irises darkened, the golden flecks in them glowing as his full attention centered on me.

My pulse jolted, and butterflies took flight in my stomach like every organ in my body wanted me to be ready for him to attack.

When he didn't come closer, my lungs worked a little easier.

"All of your pack?" Ryker clasped his hands in front of him, and his shoulders sagged. "Did you see who did it?"

I nodded but then stopped. "Not really. The Blackwood pack showed up, and I saw Reid lunge toward one of us, but I didn't see what happened after that. I...suspect they attacked us, but I don't know for sure. I didn't see anyone else, but their pack and mine run the same perimeter where our lands divide, so they could've detected intruders." Everything inside me screamed that they'd done it, but I had no proof.

I didn't understand how they could've surrounded us without any warning. We'd been patrolling the area.

Still, it had happened right after the rejection. Reid had

painted a target on my back—it couldn't be a coincidence. Even if they hadn't attacked us themselves, they must have initiated it. To me, it was one and the same, but I couldn't say that to these guys with their reputation of acting first and asking questions later.

I had every intention of discovering who'd decimated my pack. But first, I had to locate Briar and get her to a safe place.

Once I started talking, I couldn't shut up. "Someone chased Briar and me. I didn't see who, but their steps didn't sound like paws. They were in human form but ran quickly. We went to the river to hide our scents, but Briar slipped and…" *Now* my lips closed. They already knew what had happened; I didn't need to relive that horror again.

"And you're sure she's still alive?" Ryker rubbed his dark scruff.

I rolled my eyes, not bothering to hide my annoyance. "Despite what Reid proclaimed, I'm not weak, and I know what a pack link feels like." With my free hand, I patted my chest. "I feel her. She's alive." I had to hold on to that. I wasn't alone.

I closed my eyes and swallowed tears. I hated to think of Briar handling the loss of our pack alone. We should be together, supporting one another and mourning the ones we loved.

Kendric scowled, and Gage winced and glanced at Ryker and Xander. From the faint glow of their eyes, I knew what was going on. They were discussing me and my situation, and I didn't like being left in the dark.

But I no longer had a pack to discuss things with. It hit like a punch in the gut. I had no one to bounce ideas off or my dad to counsel me on what the best decision was. I was all alone despite the four people surrounding me.

"It'd be nice if you included me in the conversation." Not knowing what was going on put me more on edge. For all I knew, Ryker could be alpha-willing them to leave my ass here. Which would be fine. I just needed to know where I stood—no pun intended.

Xander lifted a hand. "We're discussing everything you told us."

"Which isn't needed." Ryker pursed his lips and shifted his weight to one side. "I'm in agreement that she should remain with us."

My heart skipped a beat, and I wasn't sure if it was from relief or fear. "What? Why?" His sudden change of heart waved red flags around like crazy in my mind. "You were ready to leave me here just moments ago."

"Yeah. Why, man?" Gage crossed his arms, emphasizing his muscular chest. "Why don't you share with the rest of the class?"

"Man, you haven't attended a class since senior year of high school." Xander side-eyed him and continued, "That was eight years ago."

"The premise applies in this situation." Gage shrugged. "So shove it."

"Now isn't the time." Kendric's nostrils flared. "Since the four of us are in agreement, let's get her back to the rental house so she can clean up while we find her something to wear."

That sounded like heaven. Maybe it was a reprieve I didn't deserve after what happened to my pack, but I couldn't walk around like this if I wanted to find Briar.

"Sounds like a plan to me." Ryker headed toward the thickening trees.

Not wanting him to change his mind—five wolves would have an easier time tracking down my sister than one

—I started to follow. But as soon as I put my weight on my legs, the world spun, and I lost my balance once more.

"Whoa." Gage's arms slipped around me, pulling me to his chest. "Don't worry, princess. As long as I'm around, I'll catch you." He winked, and I squirmed a little and looked away.

"What are you doing?" Ryker's voice had turned cold.

Holding me firmly against him, Gage responded, "Helping her. She's been through hell and isn't well."

Ryker huffed. "Then I'll carry her." Footsteps thudded toward us, and before I could tell them I was fine, I was removed from Gage's arms and tossed over Ryker's shoulder like a sack of potatoes. The food and water I'd eaten sloshed heavily in my stomach, and I swallowed, hoping to keep it down.

The worst part of it was that the shirt rode up right to the bottom of my butt cheeks. Anyone standing beside him or in front of him could get a muddy mooning at any second.

As if he could read my thoughts, Ryker placed his hand on the bottom of the shirt, anchoring it to my cheeks. When his palm touched my bare skin, heat zinged between us.

My breath caught, and I tensed. The sensation wasn't unsettling, but nothing about him should be comforting. I still didn't know why he'd changed his mind about me joining them. Something didn't add up.

The three of them seemed like decent guys, but I'd thought the same thing about Reid, and look where that landed me.

"What the hell, man?" Gage scoffed from the rear.

I didn't like the idea of wolves I didn't know or trust being behind me, but I refused to flop up and down like a fish and try to look.

Ryker didn't break pace, his stride graceful and smooth. The strength of his wolf brimmed from under his skin, and I couldn't ignore it.

I closed my eyes, not wanting to admire—er—I meant to be forced to watch his hard ass flex with each step. Even if he was sexy, his reputation had grown worse since the first attack. He'd beaten up a few people.

The group fell into silence as we continued our walk. I lifted my head, taking note of our surroundings. The trees were thinning, so I hoped that our destination was close.

"You sense something?" Xander asked. "Because I don't hear anything."

He'd asked out loud, so I assumed the question was directed at me. Great. I'd tried to be inconspicuous, but clearly, moving my head had made the other three notice me.

"No, sorry. Just trying to figure out where we are." I winced, hating being called out like that, though I understood the concern. I had just told them my pack had been wiped out, and we weren't... My breath caught. Where the hell were we?

All of a sudden, we were walking by a green picnic table, and then a door opened. Ryker carried me through the door and turned to the right. Then I was sliding down his front and being seated on a wooden chair at a circular table with three other seats.

The blood rushed from my head, and I placed my hands on the table to remain upright as he continued into the kitchen. He strolled past a small stove and opened the white refrigerator then drew out a Coke and placed it in front of me.

The other three guys entered, and Gage and Xander

took a seat on a black couch across from me as Kendric stood in front of the door with crossed arms.

"We're outside of Asheville." Kendric's jaw clenched.

It was a good thing I had my hands on the table, or I would've fallen over.

Ryker handed me the drink while saying, "About sixty miles from Shadowbrook."

"I traveled *sixty miles* from my pack lands in the river?" That was hard to believe. True, the current had been stronger than I'd remembered in years. But that meant there was a whole lot of space where Briar could be. Hell, she'd been ahead of me—she could be even farther down the river.

My eyes prickled, and my vision blurred as tears sprang up once again. Everywhere I turned, things seemed to become more hopeless. Just when I thought things were as bad as they could get, Fate gave me her middle finger all over again.

"Drink the Coke," Ryker said more gently. Some of the golden color returned to his irises, warming his eyes. "The sugar will help you feel better."

Lifting the cool can, I took a big gulp, the carbonation burning the back of my throat as the sweetness filled my mouth. Sweet drinks were one of my favorites... Well, really, anything sweet or any type of meat, but right now, this hit a spot I didn't know was there.

After guzzling about half the can, I set it down and took in my surroundings. The cabin appeared old, with paneled walls and laminate floors. It had a bathroom to the left of the kitchen and two doors across from each other that I assumed hid bedrooms. This place was small but safe and dry. The last two things were the most important.

"I'll find her something to sleep in." Gage jumped to his feet and hurried to the room on the left.

Ryker scowled at his back but remained at the table, examining my face, searching for something. I was tired of feeling like a science specimen, so I drank the rest of the Coke and then slowly climbed to my feet.

Gage reentered the room, holding a white shirt and a thin white towel. "This is all we have for you now. Write down your sizes, and one of us will run out and get you some things."

I gritted my teeth. "You don't have to do—"

"If you don't want to stand out to other supernaturals, you need to not look homeless." Ryker arched a brow. "Standing out means your location will get back to Reid or whoever attacked your pack. Do you want that?"

Though I wanted to punch him because of his tone, I clenched my hands. "I wear medium tops and underwear, size eight in pants, and a 32D bra."

"Nice." Gage smiled and winked.

My face warmed, and I grimaced. Mud cracked on my face. Snatching the two items, I carefully walked to the bathroom. Bits of mud flaked off me and onto the floor, but no one complained.

In the small bathroom, I questioned how those large men managed to move around in there. Even for me, the space was tight, but I had enough room to pull back the yellowed white shower curtain and turn on the water. I peeled off the shirt, dropped it to the cream tile floor, and stepped under the water.

Brown sludge rolled down my body, filling the bottom of the tub. I ran my hands over my skin and worked on getting every bit of mud off. After what felt like hours, I'd managed to scrub my body clean, including my hair, with a bar of Dial soap. Of course four guys would use only soap to clean their entire body, but it didn't matter. I was warm once again, my olive complexion a tad pink from the heat.

After quickly drying off, I almost felt like a person again.

Guilt nearly crushed me. Why was I alive when nearly my entire pack had died? None of it made sense.

I couldn't let my emotions distract me from my tasks. Once I found Briar, we could mourn and plan our next moves. Until then, I had to keep myself together. I was now the alpha of our two-person pack.

Running my fingers through my hair, I combed it as best I could and then put on the shirt. I almost wondered if Gage had purposely given me a white shirt, knowing the situation I'd be in. I could already tell that he was a flirt.

When I opened the door, I expected to see the four of them still in the living room. Instead, I found the couch covered in a thick blanket and a pillow.

My heart ached.

I glanced in both bedrooms. No one else was in there, and their fading scents confirmed that I was alone.

That was more than all right with me.

I climbed into my makeshift bed and went right to sleep.

I was reliving the attack on my pack. Over and over, I saw Reid lunge toward Rosa, and then I was knocked down and forced to run.

It felt like I was missing an important part of the equation, but I couldn't determine what.

Someone was chasing me.

However, this time, something felt different. Breath warmed my neck like someone was hovering over me.

Something tickled my brain, and then reality set back in.

One thing didn't change. Someone *was* watching me.

I opened my eyes, and my jaw dropped.

CHAPTER SEVEN

I froze as Ryker straightened beside my bed. My head screamed that he was going to hurt me—after all, if my fated mate could turn his back on me, why wouldn't someone like *him*?

My hand clenched, ready to throw a punch, but something he was holding caught my eye.

A purple shirt that was clearly a woman's cut.

I let out a gasp before I could stop myself.

He winced. "I didn't mean to wake you." He placed the shirt on the small table in front of me. "I just wanted to make sure your heartbeat was steady and leave out an outfit so, when you woke, you could change and get comfortable." He reached back into the bag and brought out a pack of panties.

"It's fine." I sat up quickly. Even though I'd never worn any of the items before, a man touching my underwear seemed very intimate. I didn't want to consider which one of them had picked them out, even though I had a sneaking suspicion. Nope... I would not be going there. Still, his thoughtfulness didn't fit what I knew about him. I didn't like him acting out of character; it made me unsure where I stood with him. "I can go through the bag, though I appreciate your help."

He shrugged, dropping the clothes on the floor. "Fine with me. I just didn't want you to fall and cause your healing to take longer."

Okay, that reasoning made way more sense to me and did fit what I expected from him. "Don't worry. You're not the only one ready to get going." I moved my body, waiting for the world to spin around me. Everything stayed firmly in place, and I could feel an extra jolt pulsing through my blood. I wasn't cold any longer, and I almost felt normal. "How long have I been out?"

"Twenty-four hours." Ryker rocked back on his heels. "We were beginning to worry about you, but after everything you've gone through, you probably need another day's rest before you're up to leaving. Let me make you a sandwich before you go back to sleep."

My stomach gurgled. I couldn't afford to let my emotions get the best of me. I hadn't been eating correctly since Reid had dumped me, and that last part was the least of my concerns. Right now, my goal was locating Briar and then ensuring that I took everything from Reid. Though I refused to become a murderer, that didn't mean I wouldn't find my sister and let him believe he'd won. Another thing I'd need to figure out once my sister was safely back with me.

"Eating sounds good, but I think I'm better." I tossed off the thin white sheet I'd slept under and placed my feet on the cool floor. The fact that I was commando in another man's shirt made me want to cross my arms, but that would only make the situation worse by causing the shirt to ride up higher.

He narrowed his eyes before moving around the table to the refrigerator. He pulled out some roast beef and cheese before snagging a plate and bread. "No wolf shifter could heal that quickly. I understand wanting to rush to get answers, trust me, but if you leave before you're ready, you'll only slow us down."

I gritted my teeth. I didn't appreciate him talking to me like that. He wasn't my alpha, nor did I need his permission to do anything. "And if we take too long, the trail will be cold. I need to go back and see what's left of my pack. Maybe there are clues to where Briar is, or maybe she's even waiting for me there." She'd know I'd come back searching for her and answers. "What if my sister is there and in danger because of it? Reid could be watching the area." Saying the words made my chest tighten. I knew what I'd seen, and Reid had rejected me, but our packs had always been allies. Him attacking us made no sense, but I couldn't deny what I'd witnessed.

Ryker put pieces of bread together, snagged another bottled Coke, and walked over. "I can go without you and—"

"The hell you will." I didn't trust anyone else to find my sister and keep her safe. We had only each other in this world now. We didn't know who our true allies were, and I doubted Ryker and his merry group of bandits were on our side. With what had gone down with his own pack and the royals, I had so many questions about their intent. "And I'm telling you—I might not be back to my full strength, but I *am* strong enough to go." Even if I needed to fight, I believed I could handle it now. "I wouldn't risk it otherwise." That was the truth. Even if Briar was there and had escaped notice, me coming in unable to fight if needed could be a death sentence for us both.

He handed the items to me, and I took a swig of the Coke before eating. I'd prefer water, but I understood why he was giving me soda—the sugar, calories, and caffeine.

He crossed his arms and watched me eat. I didn't like being inspected, but I also knew what he was doing—trying to prove that I wasn't fit to leave.

The sandwich was dry since he hadn't used any condiments, but I still ate it, staring him in the eye the entire time. I wouldn't cower to him or anyone, not anymore...especially not Reid. I shouldn't have run that night like a weakling. I should've done *something* when he rejected me, but I had no clue what. Everything had caught me off guard, and had I known the true consequences of tucking my tail and leaving, I would've handled it differently.

The past was the past, and I couldn't change it. But damn, I sure wished I could. The coldness from where the pack links had been made me want to shudder. Instead, I took another swig of Coke, knowing any sign of me being off balance would have Ryker riding my ass again.

Once I drained the liquid, I stood and pulled down the shirt to midthigh. I handed him the empty plate and bottle, and he arched both eyebrows. My fingers accidentally brushed his, and my stomach fluttered.

Great. Indigestion. Another problem I need right now.

He smirked as I dropped my hands, and this time, my heart skipped a beat. Hopefully, that wasn't a sign of a stroke because I could not be feeling any sort of sensations when it came to *him*.

"Anything else you need me to take off your hands?" he teased and scanned the shirt that had been loaned to me.

My face burned, but I refused to give him more of a reaction than that. "Give me a minute, and I'll have something else I need off my hands." I took the purple shirt he'd laid out and grabbed the Walmart bag before stalking toward the bathroom.

A tingling on my neck told me he was watching me the entire way, so I made sure to not miss a step. I forced myself not to slam the door shut either, not wanting him to know he was getting to me. Then I quickly dressed in the clothes they'd gotten me. Luckily, they'd bought me a bra and panties that were sealed.

The front door opened just as I rejoined Ryker. He'd already washed the dish and put it back in its place.

The other three men turned their attention to me.

"Are you sure she's well enough to go with us?" Xander's brow furrowed. "She was—"

"*She* is right here and fine." He was talking about me as if I weren't even in the room. I shook my body and straightened once more. "See?"

"All I saw was a pretty girl looking like the rhythm caught up to her poorly." Gage grimaced. "It's a damn good thing you're hot enough to pull off crazy."

Kendric hung his head while Xander just glared at Gage.

I wasn't sure how to respond to that compliment slash insult, so I pretended he hadn't said a word. "My point is if I'd done that yesterday, I'd have fallen over. The room didn't even spin an inch. I'm fine. I wouldn't do anything stupid."

"We should give you at least another few hours—" Xander started.

"If she says she's fine, then that's it." Ryker shoved his hands into his jeans pockets. "I'm not going to waste more time arguing, and honestly, the sooner we get there, the better. Remember how quickly the scents faded?" He tilted his head forward, completing the thought with his action alone.

It didn't take a brain surgeon to guess that he was referencing the night of the attack they'd escaped from.

"Fine, but she stays near me." Kendric puffed out his chest as if he expected Ryker to argue with him.

"Works for me." Ryker removed a set of keys from his pocket. "Let's get moving. We can be there in an hour and a half, right before lunch. Hopefully, if they're watching, we'll spook them into action in broad daylight so no one can easily hide in the shadows."

He did have a point there. Even though we could see well at night in our wolf forms, it was still dark and easier to hide.

My stomach dropped when I realized I had to ask for something else. "Did you, by chance, find me any shoes to wear?" They'd gotten me three pairs of jeans and shirts, but I hadn't seen any footwear.

"Yup." Gage bent and produced a bag that had been partially hidden by the sheet I'd tossed off earlier. "These."

They were cheap plastic flip-flops, but they would work perfectly if I needed to shift quickly. I could fling them off without ruining them. "Thanks. Just let me know how much I owe you so I can pay you back when I can."

"You helping us determine who slaughtered your pack will be payment enough, believe me." Ryker smiled darkly. "Now let's go." He hurried out the door without bothering to see if we followed.

I expected the guys to be right on his heels, but the three of them remained standing while the door closed.

"He's getting that weird vibe again." Gage rubbed his forehead.

Kendric nodded. "That's why I said Ember stays with me."

A lump formed in my throat as what could only be concern lined their faces. What the hell was going on? "Is there something I need to know?" If they didn't trust me around Ryker, why had we been left alone in the house?

"He won't hurt you. You don't need to worry about that." Xander grinned weakly.

That grin had dread pooling heavily in my stomach. There was something more, but they weren't going to share it with me. I wasn't their pack, after all.

We were wasting time. I slid on the flip-flops and marched out the door after Ryker. I found him unlocking a white Suburban and climbing into the driver's seat.

Within seconds, I slid into the very back of the vehicle, where I could lie down. Even though I did feel mostly better, I would take advantage of the hour-long nap I could have on my way there.

Gage sat in the passenger seat with Kendric behind him and Xander behind Ryker. As soon as everyone got settled and Ryker began driving, I lay down and closed my eyes, trying to rest.

Instead, my brain kept racing. I relived the attack and Briar's and my escape. I couldn't shake the idea that there was something strange about the attack, but I couldn't quite put my finger on it. Still, each time I remembered Reid lunging at Rosa, bile inched up and burned my throat like I might vomit.

Tears stung my eyes, but I held them back despite the coldness in my chest.

"Man, you're worrying us." Gage sighed. "You've got that scary look in your eyes you get every time we go searching."

"It's not only the four of us in here," Ryker snapped. "You shouldn't be speaking out loud."

"I wouldn't be if you hadn't locked your pack link down so we can't talk to you. I'm doing it the only way possible."

Then there was silence, which made me realize that they must have started to communicate through their pack link again. He'd rather hear what they had to say than risk me overhearing it, which made me more determined to find out what secrets they were keeping. They all seemed concerned about Ryker, but why? If they were innocent, they would share what they knew and why they hadn't been there when the royal pack and their own pack had died. Instead, no one knew anything.

I wanted to scream at the unanswered questions in my head. Maybe I shouldn't have trusted them to help me find Briar, but what other choice did I really have? I didn't have money, an ID, or a credit card. It would take time to replace some of those items, and I didn't have the means to locate Briar as easily without them.

A familiar sharp turn rocked the vehicle. One that meant we were close to my pack lands.

I expected Ryker to stop so we could walk the rest of the way, but he kept driving.

Sitting upright, I placed a hand on the back of each seat in front of me. "What are you doing? We should travel the rest on foot."

"So we have to run miles back to the car if we're attacked?" Ryker glanced in his rearview mirror. "Not happening. We need the vehicle close in case we need to get away. They're slaughtering entire packs somehow, so we need a quick escape route."

I sucked in a breath. He did have a point.

After a few more miles, the pack neighborhood came

into view. My heart seemed incapable of beating, thanks to how heavy and cold it became. I struggled enough with the memories. I hadn't expected the terror of that night to return now that I was back.

"Shit," Gage shouted. "Cover her eyes, now!"

What was he talking about? I leaned forward so I could see out the front window better…and then my heart seized in my chest.

CHAPTER EIGHT

This time, the bile surged up my throat, and there wasn't going to be any way to hold back the contents. I jerked forward, angling between the two middle-row chairs.

Kendric hurried to open the door and jumped out of the vehicle just as I started gagging. I barely made it out of the car before I began heaving by the back tire. Every time I closed my eyes, I saw the death and destruction of my pack in front of me.

Rosa's throat had been ripped out, making the image of Reid lunging at her that night pop into my head again. None of this made sense. Why would he do that? Our packs had been amicable for centuries. Yet, he was the only one near her who could have done that to her.

My chest knotted, making it hard to breathe, which made vomiting that much worse.

The front passenger seat door opened, and Gage grumbled, "We need to get her out of here."

"I'm well aware, but it's going to be a minute," Kendric replied tersely.

I didn't want them to argue because of me, but I hadn't expected to see my dead packmates. I didn't know why, but I'd assumed Reid would have taken the time to bury them. We at least deserved that. We were wolf shifters after all.

Eventually, my entire stomach emptied. Everything I'd eaten was pretty much at my feet.

More doors opened. Footsteps grew louder toward me, indicating Xander and Ryker had joined us.

I spat, trying to get the puke out of my mouth, and straightened. I didn't know what I expected to find, but it wasn't the four of them standing in a line, blocking my view of my pack home. The tightness in my chest remained, but a little bit of relief flooded my system.

"One of you go with her to the river to see if you can find any signs of what might have happened to her sister while the other three handle what's left here. She shouldn't be alone," Ryker gritted out, pressing his lips together.

Even though I probably should have examined the area with them, I didn't have the courage. My chest felt frozen while my heart ached as if it could explode or shatter at any moment. None of these people deserved this. If this was because something was wrong with me, then the attackers should've killed only me. Not everyone else.

Each breath got harder than the last, and I became light-headed. All of this was my fault, and worse, my fated mate had been the one to take everything from me. What had I done to offend Fate that I had to lose so much?

Gabe hurried over to me and slid his arm around my shoulders. He didn't flinch at the vomit below us as he guided me to the back of the Suburban. He squeezed gently. "Where did you and your sister run off to?"

Briar.

Right. I needed to locate her. "We headed to the right." I lifted my hand, gesturing toward the river.

My head began to clear, and my lungs weren't screaming like they were before. The door of the Suburban shut, and the engine turned over, informing me that the others were driving closer to the pack neighborhood. The fact that I didn't want to turn and look back at the chaos made me a coward, but if I did, I'd break down all over again. That wouldn't help me find clues to where Briar might be.

Her spot in my chest remained lukewarm, indicating that she wasn't within pack-link range. A chill ran down my spine, and I couldn't stop the shiver. She had to be in trouble, but I wasn't sure which kind—being held hostage or injured somewhere alone and unable to defend herself.

"Hey, we'll find her." Gage dropped his arm and offered a small smile. "As long as you feel her pack link, there's hope."

My heart thawed a little toward him, which caught me by surprise. *No.* I'd thought Reid was a nice person too, and look where that had gotten me. I would *not* make that mistake again. "That may be true, but what is she enduring in the meantime?" If the Blackstone pack had Briar on their land, her pack link would be warmer, and I'd be able to link with her if she was awake. The temperature of the link proved she wasn't close to where we were, so who else could be involved? My eyes burned as tears threatened to fill them.

"What's wrong?" He caught my wrist and tugged me toward him.

I blinked, not wanting to break down on him once again, and exhaled. "I really thought she'd be here." I didn't know why, and I hadn't even wanted to admit it to myself, but I had hoped that Briar and I would be reunited by now. Instead, I was no closer to finding her.

A tear trickled down my cheek, and Gage winced.

"Well, at least we know where she isn't, so that's one less place to look. Let's go see if we can determine anything else. Take me to where the two of you fell into the water."

Thunder rumbled, and I looked skyward. Dark clouds had rolled in overhead. My heart dropped to my stomach. Every time I thought things couldn't get worse, Fate proved how big of a bitch she truly was.

I yanked my wrist from Gage's grasp and ran through the oaks along the trail that we'd taken to get to the water. I breathed in the faint smell of Briar...as well as someone else. However, the second scent was nearly gone, even compared to Briar's, with a very faint musky hint that wasn't definitive. "There's a second scent, but it should be stronger than this." I wanted to stomp and scream, but all that would accomplish was alerting the Blackwood pack that I'd returned so they could try to finish what they'd started.

"That's how it was for us too." He took in a big breath. "It wasn't as faded because we arrived within thirty minutes of the attack, but there wasn't anything distinguishable about the unknown scent other than the musk."

I rubbed my head, trying to prevent the migraine that seemed determined to come.

Something hit me square on my shoulders. "Wait. You all *knew* that I'd see my pack members like that when we got here?" I lifted my chin, ready to either hear that they'd wanted me to see them like that or smell rotten eggs. If I could choose, I'd rather he be honest since my stomach still wasn't feeling right.

His jaw dropped. "Fate, no. That surprised us all. The attack on our..." He paused, closing his eyes briefly. "The bodies had all been gathered into a pile in the backyard of the royal mansion. We assumed it would be the same for your pack, but clearly, we were wrong."

I waited for the sulfur smell, but it never came. The bastard wasn't lying. Worse, I'd made him recall his own loss. "I'm sorry. I didn't—"

He lifted a hand. "Don't apologize. You did nothing wrong. We're all trying to get answers, and we're going to have to relive a lot of painful memories in order to get there."

He was right, but that didn't mean we couldn't be upset about it.

A few droplets of rain hit my face. Soon, all traces of scent and potential signs of movement would be washed away, so we'd best hurry. Not bothering to speak, I spun and headed in the direction of Shadowbrook. I could still see the paw prints from Briar and me, along with a set of footprints. No wonder the shifter hadn't been able to catch us. "The person hunting us remained in human form."

"Strange for them not to shift."

Another round of thunder rolled, but this time, it sounded closer. I picked up my pace to a jog. The rush of the river alerted me that we were getting closer, but the rain came down a little harder.

If Gage and I were pack, I wouldn't hesitate to shift so we could move faster. But we weren't, and if we were both in animal form, we wouldn't be able to communicate effectively.

When we reached the steep hill that led down to the water's edge, both of us were panting. I skidded a little on the muddy mulch due to my flip-flops, so I kicked them off. My bare feet dug into the cold, moist mulch as I carefully made my way down to the rocks. The water was running even quicker than it had been two nights ago, and it had risen higher on the embankment. I glanced at the rock where Briar had hit her head and saw a dab of dried blood.

I had the strangest urge to touch it, but I kept my hands by my sides. "She hit there."

"That's a nasty edge." Gage wrinkled his nose and stared downriver. Rain now fell steadily.

I didn't know what I'd been hoping to find here. My knees grew weak, and I wanted to curl into a ball and wake up from this nightmare.

"Let's head back to the road," Gage said, taking my hand, his warmth pushing away some of the cold I'd started feeling again.

My toes tightened around the sharp rock so I wouldn't budge from this spot. The last thing I wanted was to return and see Mom or Dad with their throats ripped out.

A sob lodged in my throat as their faces flashed inside my head. I needed to go back to my house and get pictures of them and snag my phone so I could listen to the last voicemails they'd left me. I refused to give Reid the power to prevent me from remembering their faces and voices.

"We need to go, Ember. Staying out here isn't doing us any good. We need to regroup so we can decide our next steps."

Even though I knew he was making sense, my heart didn't want to hear the message. Leaving here made things more final... something that I couldn't get back.

If Briar wasn't here, that meant something had to be preventing her from meeting me here. My legs wanted to give out. The Blackwoods must have her somewhere.

Rain pelted us, and I shivered. However, I didn't move from my spot.

He bent down and lifted me into his arms, and then he took off up the steep hill.

Even though he was a stranger, I didn't care. Someone was holding me, and that was all it took for the strangled sob to come out. I buried my face in his chest, falling apart once again. He cradled me to him, pausing only once to bend and retrieve the flip-flops I'd dropped.

For a minute, I pretended that Fate was crying along with me for everything we'd lost.

Light flashed through my closed eyelids as thunder crashed. The storm was upon us, conveying exactly the way I felt inside. I was angry, sad, and broken, needing solace in the chaos of the storm swirling around me.

Gage didn't miss a beat, hurrying back toward the town.

"I need to go inside my house," I stated, trying and failing to keep my voice steady. "I need pictures and my cell phone in case Briar tries to call me."

He sighed. "I don't think that's wise."

"I'm *not* asking. It's the first house in the neighborhood, on the right." I lifted my head, not caring if tears and snot streamed down my face. I allowed my wolf to rush forward, emphasizing my intent.

His eyes widened and he tilted his head back. "Got it. I'm talking to the others now."

I wanted to say more, but I kept my mouth shut. I chose my battles, and it wasn't worth having one now if they didn't try to keep me from my house.

Gage's footsteps held steady, and before long, they rang against a more solid surface. We'd made it to my driveway. He didn't pause, and I didn't raise my head, not wanting to see the disaster around us.

When a door opened and the smell of home hit my nose, I lifted my gaze. He breezed through the kitchen, and

I glanced into the living room and saw the blanket Mom always used while sitting on the couch heaped on the floor. The television flickered, though there was no sound. Dad must have muted the television instead of turning it off before running out to face the threat head-on.

"Where's your room? We need to hurry. This is going to piss Ryker off. He didn't want you brought here."

In fairness, I didn't think I could handle being inside for long.

He set me down, and I took off toward my room. I headed straight to my closet and removed a duffel bag then filled it with clothes, essentials, and everything else I could fit. Then I swiped my cell phone and charger from my nightstand, knowing I had enough pictures and voicemails on there to last until I could come back for everything else.

I marched across the hall to Briar's room and grabbed similar stuff for her. She'd need it when we located her. I had to hold on to the belief that we would find her and make it back home.

Gage watched from the hallway. When I exited Briar's room, he asked, "Are you ready to go?"

I nodded. Being here was painful. I kept expecting my parents to walk into the house and check on me any minute.

"When we go out the back door, look at the car, nothing else. They cleared the area in case we needed to rush back to the vehicle, so you shouldn't see anything if you don't search for it. The door's unlocked—we're just going down the road to wait until they're done." He took Briar's teal bag and my maroon one from me.

I grimaced. Even though I didn't want to see the bodies, I couldn't just *leave* them. "I need to bury my pack. They deserve a place to rest."

"Ryker is taking care of that. He and the others are

already digging a hole. Wait here, and I'll go help them. We'll leave a marker so you'll know where they're buried."

I hated that, but at least my pack and family would be returned to the earth. We weren't sure if we were safe, and the fact that Ryker was taking the time to bury them without me asking meant a lot to me.

I was surprised that Ryker had led that effort.

"Don't worry. I don't have any desire to see anything else." Rosa's body would forever haunt me, her skin pale and dark, congealed blood coating her neck and the grass beneath her. Nausea curdled in my stomach once again, so I thought through the recipe of an Oreo pound cake I'd wanted to try to make.

When we hit my backyard, I homed in on the Suburban, not even blinking in case I accidentally looked away from it.

The two of us hurried to the vehicle, and I opened the back door and slid into the far back seat, ducking out of the rain. The trunk opened, and I glanced back as Gage threw in the two duffel bags.

Ryker slid into the driver's seat, and both back doors opened, Kendric and Xander climbing in as well. Mud covered Ryker's clothes and hands, and dabs of it dotted his face from digging the huge grave. Gage jogged to the front like he was in a hurry.

There was no way he'd taken care of all one hundred members of my pack so soon. "I thought you were going to bury them—"

Ryker's dark gaze flickered to the rearview mirror, catching my eye. "We were, but there's been another attack."

CHAPTER NINE

My mouth dried out, and I forgot how to breathe. "Another attack?" There had been three attacks in the past few months, so a fourth happening this soon startled me. Had I misunderstood?

Ryker exhaled as he threw the vehicle into reverse and punched the gas. The tires squealed against the wet asphalt, and the stench of burned rubber filled my nose, upsetting my stomach once again.

I swallowed, desperate to not vomit again.

"Did she fall down and hit her head?" Ryker grumbled loud enough for me to hear but then spoke clearer. "Yes, that's what I said. There's been another attack."

My gut clenched. "What pack? If another pack assisted Briar, then she could be in danger." Would Reid have hunted my sister down to kill her when I was still alive and walking around? If he knew she'd survived, then he should've figured out I had as well. "We need to hurry and get there before they harm her."

He shifted the Suburban into Drive, spun around in the

grass, and took off. "I doubt that's what happened. That wouldn't make any sense."

The way he completely disregarded my concerns had my hands balling into fists. "Because all the other attacks have." I didn't like being talked down to, and I didn't give a damn if he was the alpha of the Grimstone pack. He could kiss my ass. "Thanks for clearing that up for me."

Kendric and Xander glanced at each other uncomfortably as Gage turned his head back and gave me a slight nod.

"We're the ones *helping* you," Ryker seethed. "Don't forget that."

"Don't worry, I'm completely aware, and besides, I'd doubt you'd ever risk letting me." I knew better than to trust this pack.

His hands clenched on the steering wheel so hard that his knuckles turned white enough for me to notice from back here. I hated that he'd thrown my dependency on them in my face. However, the decision had been made, and I couldn't do a damn thing about it now.

I needed to find a way out of here. I didn't want to be with a group of people who would consistently make sure I knew I was the outsider and act like my questions and concerns weren't valid. A lot of other packs operated like that, but mine didn't, and now that it had only two members, both female, I wouldn't stand for that sort of treatment.

I glanced at the side windows, which were opened only a smidgen. There was no way in hell I would be able to fit through the cracks. Even if I could, I wouldn't do that...at least, not yet. And if another pack was getting slaughtered, the last thing I wanted to do was hinder us from reaching them in time.

Swallowing my pride, I sat back in the seat with my

arms crossed. My skin crawled with the realization that I'd once again left my pack without a proper burial.

My chest ached again as the coldness of the lost pack links amplified, reminding me that, if something happened to my sister, I'd be a rogue wolf. My wolf whimpered in my head. If I lost her, I wasn't sure what would become of me. I'd continue on because I'd refuse to let Reid have the illusion of a win out of spite. But the mere thought of Briar not coming home had my heart throbbing.

Gage's eyes glowed, and he scowled, no doubt pack-linking with the others so I couldn't overhear. That was fine with me. I wasn't part of their pack, nor did I want to be. I was better off by myself.

I watched the trees whip by the windows, causing a little bit of dizziness to wash over me. I'd rather take the discomfort than stare out the front and see the four of them. Maybe I was being fickle, but I didn't give a damn.

The ride was quiet, and I didn't waste my breath to ask where we were heading. I leaned my head back and closed my eyes, trying to center myself. A tornado of anger, pain, and loss ravaged my soul, and an extra bolt of energy that hadn't been there before ran through my blood. It must be the alpha power transfer from my dad.

The realization made me feel as if I were drowning despite being surrounded by oxygen. All these changes were overwhelming, and I wasn't sure of what type of person I'd be when everything settled. For now, my entire focus had to be on locating Briar and taking her somewhere safe and sound.

Wind swooshed past the windows, and my body swayed with each curve of the road. I'd hoped that the pressure behind my eyes would ease, but the farther away I got from my pack home, the lonelier I felt as the reality of the situation sank in.

A seat belt unbuckled, and I opened my eyes to find Xander climbing back toward me. He plopped to my left, his body pressing into my side.

I lifted my chin, refusing to cower. There were four of them to my one, but they were already throwing my need for their help in my face. I would not make the situation even worse, especially since I wasn't nearly as injured as before.

"Are you okay?" Xander asked. "You seem—"

"You're actually asking me that?" My voice came out louder than I intended, but damn. What an asinine question. "We just left my slaughtered pack behind unburied, and I'm no closer to locating my sister. Not only that but right now, another pack is going through exactly what happened to me a few nights ago. Do you actually expect me to be okay?"

He grimaced, dissipating a fraction of my anger, then sighed. "That's fair, and it was a stupid question. We're just in a hurry to get to Asheville to help the vampires."

My head jerked back. "Vampires?" Out of all possible scenarios, that hadn't crossed my mind. Though wolf shifters and vampires didn't hate one another, we never sought each other's company. "We left my pack unburied to help *vampires*?" Rage returned with a vengeance.

"*We?*" Ryker glared at me through the mirror once more. "There was no *we* back there, princess. It was Xander, Kendric, and me."

"Dammit, Ryker." Gage smacked the glove box. "Don't you remember how it was for us? We weren't able to bury the dead for a week. It's only been two days for her, and she doesn't have any of her pack to lean on. You've got to stop being such a dick."

I expected Ryker to snap back, but he remained silent. Somehow that was more uncomfortable than if he'd responded in kind.

Tears pricked my eyes, and I inhaled deeply, trying to hold them back. I couldn't fall apart, but I hadn't expected Gage to risk upsetting his alpha for me. His loyalty could change in a second, especially if Ryker used alpha will on him. I'd heard rumors that the Grimstone alphas would use their power against their pack when necessary, making pack members do things against their free will.

Gage arched a brow at Ryker, daring him to do or say something. When nothing happened, Gage turned to me. "I know it doesn't seem that we should be abandoning your pack, especially with the rain washing away any lingering scent traces, but after the wolves turned their backs on us, the vampires extended an olive branch. They let us stay with them while we got our feet back underneath us."

My eyes widened. "What do you mean—they took you in?"

"They helped us when your pack and the others wouldn't," Ryker cut in. That cold, dark gaze met mine in the rearview mirror. "That's all you need to know. The attack on them will leave behind fresh scents, which will be stronger than anything we could pick up in your pack territory."

Xander gestured to the window. "Not necessarily in this rain."

From the edge around the seat, I noticed Kendric tense. During my short time with them, I'd already determined that he was the least talkative of the group, but he hadn't said a word at all and seemed even more on edge than the rest of us.

"Do you want us to turn around and head back then?" Ryker spat and lifted a brow in a challenge.

Jaw clenching, Xander rolled his shoulders back. "I didn't say that. All I was trying to get across was that we shouldn't get our hopes up. There's been a ton of rain with the storm. Of course we need to show up. We need to help the nest if we're able. We owe them."

Silence filled the air once more, and Xander stayed in the back next to me. Our legs barely touched, but it was enough for me not to feel quite as alone.

Every few minutes, the base of my neck tingled. Each time it happened, I'd look forward and notice Ryker quickly glancing away as if trying to hide that he'd been watching me.

Another fifteen minutes passed, and we pulled into Shadowbrook.

The town was the closest one to where I lived, a mere twenty minutes away. If he could treat his fated mate the way he had, the very person Fate had chosen perfectly for him, then maybe he's capable of treating all of the supernatural species, including the wolves, the same way. Had Reid stalked the vampires and decided to take them out next? Only wolf shifters had been attacked up to this point.

The houses grew closer together as we approached the city limits. The rain continued to pelt down on us as Ryker turned and drove between the various brick buildings that made up downtown, passing small merchant stores, restaurants, bars, and clubs that would be busy tonight once the rain had passed. They were different sizes but connected to each other block over block.

Right by the brick building of the biggest club were the

two vampire houses. About ten vampires lived in each so they could feed off the tourists easily while remaining hidden in plain sight by appearing human. Each two-story house was made of gray brick and had a steeply sloped rooftop that gave off a gothic vibe. The front door to the last house, farthest from the main strip, was open.

A shifter in animal form wouldn't have been able to open that huge door, and a vampire would have been able to smell them coming.

Ryker pulled up in front of the house and parked, and the five of us climbed out. A scream cut off short like the person had died.

Kendric didn't pause, racing toward the house.

Ryker's gaze landed on me, and he shook his head. "Hell no. You're staying in the Suburban."

I laughed, knowing that we didn't have time for this argument. Not only was time of the essence, but we were getting drenched. "I'm going in and finding proof that Reid is behind the attacks." The Blackwood pack was respected, so if I was going to accuse them of slaughtering my pack, I would need evidence. Otherwise, I would appear like a scorned lover trying to get revenge.

That was the last thing I needed.

"You two need to stop this. Can't you smell the blood?" Gage gestured to the house. "There's an attack going on." Then he raced toward the house with Xander by his side.

I stepped to follow when Ryker's hand grabbed mine.

"You were severely injured—" He started, but a scream cut him off.

The two of us took off toward the house.

We ran through the front arched double doors and straight into the living room, almost slamming into Gage and Xander. The inner walls were gray stone with a curved staircase ascending to the left.

A woman with dark hair lay sprawled on the floor behind a black leather sectional couch. The copper scent of blood hit my nose along with the sickeningly sweet signature smell of vampire, which overrode the faint musk indicating shifters once again. I still couldn't make out anything distinctive.

Kendric was nowhere to be found, but the four of us rushed to the woman on the floor. Her chest barely moved, although her heart was still beating. Blood gushed from her neck, but her throat hadn't been completely ripped out.

"Annabelle," Gage gasped, kneeling beside her. He took her hand in his. "You're going to be all right."

She made a gurgling sound, and the corners of her lips curved upward. "Bad..." she rasped, her words almost inaudible "...liar."

"I'll go find human blood for her." Xander hurried out the front door.

"No time," she slurred, but he couldn't hear her. He had to be searching for someone to bring back here.

"We have to try something. We can't just let you die." Gage's brows furrowed, and he clutched her hand tighter.

But even as he tried to reassure her, her skin grew sallow before my eyes. Blood pulsed from her neck wound, dripping between the fingers of the hand she was using to put pressure on it.

"Who did this to you?" Ryker stood on her other side, arms crossed.

She opened her mouth to respond, but her breath caught, and then she wheezed, filling her lungs once more.

It sounded like the death rattle my grandmother made

moments before she died. This woman didn't have much longer.

"Dammit, Annabelle." Ryker squatted, shaking her arm. "Who did this to you? What did you see? We need answers."

"Ryker, stop." Gage's brows furrowed. "She's struggling. Don't push her until she's more recovered."

"We don't have time for that." Ryker bared his teeth. "She's not going to make it. She needs to tell us what she can before she dies."

My heart ached. Right now, Annabelle needed comfort and to be around people who cared for her. I understood Ryker's desperation to know who'd attacked her, but based on what I'd seen the night my pack was killed, I suspected I knew who it was, though I still had a hard time wrapping my head around it. And she was losing strength fast.

She opened her mouth, but all that came out was an even deeper rattle.

Ryker leaned over her and placed his ear by her mouth. "Tell me again."

Her lips moved, though I couldn't hear anything beyond the rattle, and then her heart stopped, and her chest deflated. Her hand slackened, falling to the floor.

Death had taken her.

"Son of a bitch." Ryker's face contorted in rage. "I should've known."

My heart skipped a beat. Annabelle had managed to tell him. "Did she confirm it was Reid?"

CHAPTER TEN

His face flushed, and some sort of film shimmered over his eyes. I blinked. Each time I opened my eyes again, the sheen remained.

He straightened up as his nostrils flared. "She said to find and protect Adira. I couldn't make out a damn word after that. Anything she knew about her attackers died along with her."

"Ryker," Gage gritted out as he leaned over the vampire, placing her hands by her sides like he was trying to make her more comfortable. "What's the plan? A lot of vampires have died."

My heart squeezed uncomfortably at his tenderness. At one time, I'd expected Reid to be kind like that, but I'd learned that anyone outside my pack could turn on me so quickly I'd get whiplash. The wall around my heart hardened once again. I had to remember that I couldn't trust anyone but myself.

"I'm going to check the perimeter since Kendric went upstairs." Xander walked around Annabelle's head, his brows creased in concern. "Do you wanna come with me?" His eyes flicked toward mine.

"She stays with me." Ryker cut the air with one hand. "You two see if you can catch a trail out back while Ember and I go out front. I need you to focus on our task, not sniff around her."

I wanted to roll my eyes. He intended to watch my every move, and I was certain he didn't like the way his pack tended to protect me from him. Still, his concern wasn't for my safety. Ryker was smart and knew that if the attackers did have Briar, I was the person most likely to locate them due to the packmate connection I had with my sister.

"Fine." Xander didn't hesitate to rush to the door.

Gage jumped to his feet and paused like he was considering arguing, but before he could speak, Ryker took my wrist and led me out the front door.

Not wanting to waste time, I didn't argue. Ryker and I were at least in agreement on one thing—we needed each other. I needed him to help retrieve my sister, and he needed me to find more answers.

I hadn't noticed any strong scents inside, but I'd hoped that was due to the overpowering vampire blood. The two of us slipped through the front door as a chill racked my body. I searched the area for signs of somebody watching us, but I didn't see anything as the rain continued to fall. The only sounds were the handful of passing cars and the spatter of rain on the rooftops.

The air held a slight hint of musk, indicating wolves once again, but I couldn't identify anything distinct about it. I rocked back on my heels as the rain hit my face. "How is this even possible? They were *just* here."

A muscle in Ryker's jaw flexed. "I know. This is exactly what it was like when we got back to our pack and the royals. I'd hoped that your pack situation would be different, given how Reid acted, but it wasn't. I don't understand how any of this is possible."

A strong breeze picked up, taking more scents away with it, but the sensation of being watched didn't go away. I hated it when I got paranoid, but the air seemed to hold a warning.

Ryker didn't seem to notice as he headed over to the corner of the yard, sniffing. Even though he was in human form, I could see the faint glow of his wolf coming to the surface.

Something inside me responded, and my feet moved closer to him of their own accord, without permission from me.

"Son of a bitch." Ryker's voice was guttural, his eyes returning to normal, but the weird sheen over them was somehow even more visible. "I don't understand how they're doing this."

When his face tightened and his jaw clenched, my feet stilled. Whatever had flared inside me was gone. Luckily, there was still about ten feet between us.

I understood his frustration. Without proof that Reid engineered these attacks, no one would believe us. Not after Reid had shamed me in front of everyone, and especially not now that I was associated with Ryker and his pack of merry men. I would look like a woman scorned who got herself to believe in something that wasn't real. "How the hell are we supposed to prove Reid's behind it all so that we can punish him and his pack?"

"We need to figure out who the fuck Adira is and locate your sister." He shook his head as we headed around the building toward the side of the road. "For them to attack like this, they had to be somewhat in the open. I don't—" His eyes flashed with a pack link connection, and then he took off running toward the back of the house.

My heart dropped as I wondered what could possibly be wrong now. Refusing to be left behind, I sprang into action and moved quicker than I expected. When I rounded the corner of the stone house, Ryker was approaching Xander and Gage, who had a man in their grasps. The sweet smell informed me the man was a vampire.

"Let me go," he gritted out as he twisted in their hold, trying to get his arms free. "I was heading into town." Wavy hair fell over dark eyes, the irises outlined in crimson—proof he'd recently drunk his fill.

"Oh, we are aware." Xander fisted the hair at the back of his head. "We saw you scrambling out of the crawl space."

Ryker threw a punch to one side of the vampire's skull. The vampire's eyes rolled back, and his head slumped forward to hang limply.

"Tie him up with the rope in the back of the Suburban and put him in the trunk." Ryker marched toward the back of the house like he was on a mission.

My mouth dropped open as I stumbled back several feet. "What the *hell*?" I couldn't have seen what I just saw. Yet the poor man's head hung loosely, emphasizing that he had, in fact, been knocked unconscious.

Xander and Gage grimaced but began dragging the vampire toward the Suburban.

They were actually going to obey Ryker's command.

"You can't be serious," I muttered, watching Ryker slam the back door as he went into the house. A part of me wanted to follow him to see what he was up to, but it was for the best that I remained outside, especially after seeing how the one vampire died.

Images of Rosa appeared in my head, and bile churned

in my stomach once more. Still, I had one task I could focus on that wouldn't result in me falling apart again, so I jogged in front of Xander and Gage, blocking their path.

"We don't have a choice." Gage lifted a brow. "He'll alpha-will us if we don't obey orders. Either way, Simon here ends up in the same situation. The only difference is whether the two of us also have to deal with Ryker's annoyance when we try to disobey."

My breath caught. Dad had used alpha will very sparingly and only used it more frequently since the whole debacle with Reid. In fact, before that, I remembered only one occurrence in my entire lifetime, and that had been when a member of our pack, Steve, had wanted to attack another wolf for taking the woman he wanted to mate with. Dad had decreed that Steve had to obey the woman's decision, and he'd left our pack shortly after that.

Obviously, Ryker didn't have an issue using alpha will anytime he wanted to.

"If *I* let him go—" I started.

"It'll be worse for Simon if you do that." Gage placed his free hand on my shoulder. "If Ryker believes he knows something, he'll just hunt him down. His scent would be fresh too."

"So what? At least he'll have a chance to escape." I doubted this poor guy who'd just endured an attack would be willing to tell us anything after Ryker had punched him out.

Xander snorted. "He's unconscious. There'll be no escaping. Besides, do you want our help locating your sister?"

Yes. Yes, I did. And they did have a point about the vampire being passed out...

Even though the last thing I wanted to do was help

kidnap the man, I made my way to the Suburban and popped the trunk open for them. I refused to tie the vampire up, but I wasn't angry at Xander and Gage. Their hands were metaphorically tied ...unlike the way Simon's would be soon.

After a few minutes, they had Simon bound and shoved into the trunk with the door closing when Ryker and Kendric came out of the house three doors down. Their expressions were strained, and Kendric had blood on his shirt.

"We're heading out," Ryker announced, and all of us climbed into the vehicle.

The stench of blood and vampire had already saturated the Suburban before we pulled out of the driveway. Kendric had his phone out, typing some sort of message, and I sat in the back, glancing over my shoulder to watch Simon's head bob at each bump.

Even though I knew the answer, I had to hear it from Ryker and Kendric. I swallowed, bracing myself for the truth. "Were there any survivors?"

Somehow the silence felt heavier than if they'd already said the words. Gage looked back at me, the skin around his eyes tight.

I hated it when people treated me like a delicate flower. They just needed to be straight and say the words. "Were they all dead?" I asked again but louder.

Of course, it was Ryker who rasped, "Yes." The word was deep and heavy with pain that I understood within my own heart. A little bit of my anger toward him ebbed, though I still couldn't believe what he'd done to the poor, innocent man behind me.

Kendric rubbed his temples. I imagined what he'd seen

was worse than my dead pack. Somehow, that knowledge sat bitter on my tongue.

"Raven will be okay, man," Xander said as he reached over and patted Kendric's arm. "She's dealt with loss before."

"True, but I hate that another of her friends was taken from her." Kendric dropped the phone into his lap and shook his head. "She's lost so many people in her life."

"We all have." Ryker cleared his throat. "Don't forget that."

"None of us have forgotten that, man," Gage snapped, jerking in Ryker's direction. "You act as if we aren't all suffering the same as you, but we are."

Ryker's hands tightened on the wheel, his knuckles blanching. "Doesn't seem like it. None of you are focused on finding the attackers who murdered the royals and our pack after sending us on some bogus mission so we looked like we were either cowards or behind it."

My breath caught. I hadn't intended to cause such a harsh atmosphere. Yet the hair on the back of my neck continued to rise, and I glanced behind me to confirm that the vampire was still unconscious.

"We're driven to find them just as much as you are." Xander wrinkled his nose. "Just because we're also worried about others outside our pack doesn't mean that our goals aren't aligned."

"Distractions allow the trail to get colder. We have to be able to move at a moment's notice." Ryker shook his head. "We just arrived at the vampires, but the scents might as well have been hours old. We can't be days behind."

The other three leaned back in their seats, becoming quiet. My mind reeled as I realized that, even though they were a pack, they weren't fully united in their objectives.

The incident in question clearly had driven a wedge between them instead of bringing them closer together—it seemed tragedy had a funny way of making relationships take an extreme turn for better or worse.

I tossed my feet onto the other end of the back seat and leaned against the door. I didn't want to chance the vampire waking up and somehow finding a way out of his restraints then attacking us before we arrived at our destination. Wherever that was.

Leaning my head back, I closed my eyes and focused on the sounds of the vehicle—the purring of the engine and the breathing of each one of us in the vehicle. Images of my pack tried to pop into my head, and I nearly gave myself over to the crushing pain. However, I couldn't lose myself right now. Not with them.

Pushing away my loss was the hardest thing I'd ever had to do, so to help, I focused on the faintly warm spot in my chest.

Briar.

The reason I remained with this pack. They had agreed to help me, and if Ryker didn't follow through on his words, I wouldn't hesitate to leave.

After what felt like hours, the vehicle slowed, and I opened my eyes to see that we'd pulled onto a gravel road surrounded by woods. It took me only a moment to recognize where we were—Shadowbrook National Park—but the setting sun meant that the park was closed.

"What are we doing here?" I asked.

"We're going to get some answers." Ryker got out and slammed his door shut. He marched around to the back of the Suburban, but the other three didn't move from their spots.

I dropped my feet back onto the floorboard just as the

trunk opened. Ryker reached down and tossed the vampire over his shoulder like he didn't weigh two hundred pounds.

"And exactly—" I started, but he shut the trunk and headed into the woods. When the guys stared at the ground and didn't move, I realized they knew what was going on. I finished my question. "How does he plan on doing that?"

"It's best if you don't know." Gage rubbed the back of his neck and remained facing forward.

I tensed. "No. He wouldn't." I'd heard rumors of how Ryker interrogated people, but I'd hoped it was blown out of proportion. Yeah, he hadn't seemed friendly to me, but he had saved me. Torture was a whole different level.

When the other three didn't respond, I got to my feet and shoved in between the middle-row seats. Torturing people, especially fresh victims, was beyond cruel—it was inhumane, and I wouldn't stand for it.

"Whoa." Xander grabbed my arm, trying to prevent me from edging past him and out the door. "It's best if you stay here with us. Trust me."

Those words alone made me even more determined to go. I growled, "You can either let me out the easy way or I'll fight and still get out the hard way." I didn't care if he was a man with five inches of height on me. "You pick."

"Let her go," Gage said. "Someone needs to try to reason with him, and the three of us can't."

Pursing his lips, Xander seemed to be trying to decide what to do next. "Fine." He moved so I could get out the door.

I rushed after Ryker. I couldn't see him anymore, but I could smell him clearly and hear the burble of a stream. I jogged to catch up...and then I heard something sickening.

I broke through two oaks to see what was causing the noise, and it was even worse than I'd thought.

CHAPTER ELEVEN

My mouth opened, and I froze, trying to process what I was seeing. The vampire lay on his stomach against the rocky embankment with Ryker straddling his waist, his arms looped through Simon's so the vampire couldn't move them. He submerged Simon's head in the shallow yet gushing water while the vampire kicked and bucked, trying to throw Ryker off without any success.

I dashed toward them. "What are you *doing*?" My voice came out way higher than I intended, but I had never seen anyone being tortured before. Dad never used these tactics.

"Finding out everything he knows." Ryker didn't bother looking my way, completely fixed on his task.

"How can he tell you anything if he's dead?" I reached their side and clutched Ryker's arm, trying to yank him off Simon. "Let him breathe."

"He's a vampire, Ember." Ryker's head lifted while Simon continued to struggle. "He can stay underwater longer than us, you know that. And believe me, he won't tell us shit if I don't torture him." The sheen over his eyes had thickened as if the moon was reflecting on his irises even though the real moon had risen behind him.

My hand dropped, and I stumbled back. How was that even possible?

At that moment, Simon's thrusts lost some force, so Ryker fisted the hair on the back of his head and lifted.

Water sluiced from Simon's face as he coughed and took huge gasps of air. He sputtered, "Why are you doing this to me? Just kill me and get it over with."

"I'm not going to *kill* anyone right now." Ryker clenched his jaw. "Stop deflecting. I want to know who attacked the vampires tonight."

"If I told you, you would definitely kill me." Simon's face twisted with disgust.

Without hesitation, Ryker pressed Simon's face into the water once again.

The vampire thrashed wildly, and my heart broke. This man had just endured an attack that had ended in the deaths of his friends, if not his family, and he was being tortured by the person they'd called for help against their attackers.

This time, I wrapped both hands around Ryker's arm and yanked. "You're no better than the ones who attacked our packs and the vampires!" I hated that my strength hadn't completely returned. Still, even without tapping into my still-weak magic, I'd managed to yank hard enough for Ryker to lean in my direction.

"Maybe not," he spat, and the veins in his arm bulged as he straightened. "But it's the only way we're going to get answers from him."

This wasn't right. Why would anyone want to share information with us after being treated so horribly? "You didn't even try to talk to him! How can you possibly know that?" Back at the vampire houses, Gage and Xander had already detained Simon because he'd tried to run away. Then Ryker had showed up and immediately treated Simon like a prisoner and not a victim.

"Just trust me." He narrowed his eyes at me.

I scoffed bitterly. *Trust* him. I didn't trust anyone but myself and Briar. That had been a recent and hard lesson that would stick with me forever.

His brows rose ever so slightly like he hadn't expected that reaction.

Good. Screw him. I wouldn't tuck my tail between my legs, nor could I be forced to obey him because he wasn't *my* alpha.

His eyes glowed, enhancing the unusual sheen, and I knew what he was doing—calling the rest of his pack.

If I were going to attempt something, I needed to do it now and quickly before the others arrived. This time, I yanked at my wolf, borrowing some of her strength. I'd hoped I wouldn't need to tap into my magic yet since neither my human nor my animal side was at full strength, but I couldn't allow Ryker to continue torturing somebody.

Before I could change my mind, I raised my arms, causing his eyes to widen. He shifted his grasp, but before he could fight off my attack, I shoved him in the shoulder. He wasn't prepared for my strength, expecting me to be weak based on my previous attempts to take him down, and he wasn't able to offset the motion.

He grunted as his side hit the ground, and I used my leg to remove his from Simon's waist.

"Stop," he rasped, rolling over to his knees.

The vampire lifted his head from the water and crawled away. He coughed as he tried to stand, but Ryker spun around and kicked him in the back. The vampire fell forward onto his knees again, his hands splashing as he used the riverbed to keep his face out of the water.

I'd hoped that my sudden burst of strength would've had a larger impact on Ryker, but I should've known better. He was a strong wolf after all.

I jumped over Simon, and Ryker turned toward me and raised his arms to stop my momentum, so I changed my approach and tapped into my wolf again. As his hands gripped my waist, I punched him in the jaw.

His head snapped sideways, and he stumbled back.

"Run!" I exclaimed and threw all my weight onto Ryker, sending him sprawling.

My body jerked as I landed on him, and a few rocks scattered at the impact.

Footsteps pounded behind us, and an overly sweet-scented breeze curled past me as a few drops of water hit my arm.

A little bit of the tension left my body. Simon had gotten away.

My relief was short-lived. Ryker's massive hands grasped my arms and shoved me off him. My body flew through the air before I landed hard on my side. Sharp pain radiated down my shoulder as Ryker climbed to his feet.

His face was flushed, and his nostrils flared as he sniffed the air. "You have no fucking clue what you've done. You better hope like hell I can find him." Though vampires ran quicker than us, they couldn't sustain their speed for long periods, and their overly sweet smell lingered in the air longer than that of other supernaturals.

"I stopped you from torturing someone who just lost *everything*." My voice cracked on the last word. I understood exactly how Simon had to be feeling. He'd lost everyone in that house like I'd lost my pack, and I still was barely functioning despite not having been tortured right afterward.

I stood, ignoring the ache in my shoulder, refusing to allow him to continue to look down his nose at me.

Bastard.

I'd never been able to stand the alphaholes in other packs who seemed to believe they were superior to not only their packmates but all others as well. They had an arrogance that caused anger to boil inside them, which was one reason that my pack had kept to ourselves as much as possible.

Ryker didn't even flinch, but his face set into deep grooves, conveying his disgust. "You know *nothing*," he snapped and vanished between two large oak trees, chasing the vampire.

My heart ached, and I fisted my hands at my sides. Other than causing frustration and anger, his reaction shouldn't affect me, so feeling anything else should not be possible.

Unprocessed grief. That was what had to be making my emotions all crazy, and it clearly had nothing to do with *him*. However, I needed to keep the emotions at bay until I located my sister. That was the reason I was here with Ryker; I had to remember that.

A cold, heavy knot dropped into my stomach. What if he decided I wasn't worth keeping around and I had to locate my sister on my own? I knew, without a doubt, after what I'd just witnessed, that going it alone could be a death sentence for not only me but my sister too.

I was about to go after him when Gage, Kendric, and Xander jogged into view.

All three wore varying degrees of a frown, with Kendric's scowl being by far the deepest. He gestured to me and said, "Xander, stay with her while Gage and I go after Ryker."

Xander's head tilted back. "What? Why me? I should be part of the hunt."

"That right there is why." Gage shook his head and didn't slow down even a step, rushing past me to follow Simon and Ryker's trail. "You don't know how to keep your mouth shut."

Huffing, Xander stopped in front of me and pursed his lips. "I guess I get babysitting duty."

I lifted my chin, ignoring the burn of the muscles in my injured shoulder. "I don't need babysitting. That's insulting."

He arched a brow. "Says the woman who ran while her pack got murdered, lost her sister, almost drowned, and now pissed off the one alpha who is the most driven to find her missing sister's captors."

His words echoed the same fear that sat uncomfortably within me. I hated feeling exposed and worthless, but ever since I'd been rejected by my fated mate in front of hundreds of shifters, I seemed to keep finding myself in worse and worse situations...something no true alpha would experience. Not that my sister or I had a choice now of who would lead the two of us. I was stronger than her, and my wolf would never be able to submit to hers even if she made the most sense as a leader.

Still, I refused to appear weaker than I already did to all of them. "I couldn't stand by and let him torture someone like that. It's not *right*. That vampire almost got killed after surviving an attack on his nest. How can you even try to justify that?"

He straightened, but his shoulders drooped. "I can't, but I don't have much choice right now with how Ryker's acting. I keep hoping he'll snap out of *this* and go back to normal."

My hands relaxed, and I tilted my head. "Normal?"

"Yeah. He's only been like this since our pack—" He cut himself off as his face twisted into what could only be described as agony.

He didn't need to finish the statement because my heart shattered all over again. I knew exactly what he was going to say because he looked like I imagined I did whenever I thought about my own pack. "He wasn't like this before?" I arched a brow, daring him to contradict me. Even before the royal and protector packs were slaughtered, there'd been so many stories about the way the Grimstone pack handled threats. They had no issues with torturing, starving, cage fighting, and beating individuals to get information or make a point, which was what I'd just witnessed from Ryker.

Xander's head jerked back. "You'd know if I were lying. Why would you even ask that?"

He was right. There was no hint of sulfur in the air...but none of this made sense to me. However, my end goal was unchanged—find my sister. "It doesn't matter. We just need to start searching for answers again instead of wasting time hunting down a vampire."

Every second that passed could put my sister's life more at risk. My only comfort was that the connection was still present. If we didn't get a lead soon, I'd have to shift into my wolf and focus purely on our connection to locate her. It would be long and tedious with the connection so faint, but it might be better than what we had, which was *nothing*.

"The one thing we've learned since *that* day is once Ryker is set on something, there's no deterring him. He'll alpha-will us the second we don't listen, making things even more tense."

The more I learned about Ryker, the more it validated my opinion of him. He was an arrogant know-it-all who could cost me locating my sister. But whoever I was up against had slaughtered two packs and a massive vampire nest, which made it clear that going alone would essentially be a death sentence for me.

Maybe they were using my sister to lure me somewhere so they could finish us both off.

"I made the right call." I crossed my arms, ignoring my aching shoulder. "You can't just torture someone like that, especially after what he witnessed. It's inhumane."

"I don't know." He shrugged. "Ryker is trying to get justice for our pack, and I can't blame him at all."

Huffing, I dropped my arms. Talking to him was a waste of energy, and I didn't have much to spare. Ryker was his alpha, so even if Xander agreed with me, he couldn't do a damn thing about it. "So we're just stuck here until they've captured Simon or they tire of searching for him?" If they didn't get their shit together, I'd have to go off alone and hope for the best.

"Yes, because if *we*"—he pointed at himself and then me —"keep interfering, it's going to make things take longer, so just sit tight and stop causing problems."

Problems? Yes, me saving someone from torture was such an *issue.*

Not bothering to tell Xander where I was heading, I spun on my heels and marched back to the vehicle. There was no point in standing there, and now that the adrenaline from my outburst was wearing off, I realized how much energy I'd used. My legs were harder to lift with every step, but I gritted my teeth and kept going.

I took a deep breath and glanced at the now-dark sky. Another day gone with no leads on Briar. My heart ached, and the chill in my chest seemed to grow colder. Only the deep ache left reminded me that something pleasant used to be there. Even Briar's faint link reminded me that I could lose everyone I loved. She was just out of reach.

A vise tightened around my heart, squeezing to the point that I thought it would implode.

My blood tingled through my body, and my head screamed that something strange and different was hiding about fifty feet ahead of me deep within the woods. But that didn't make sense. There were no sounds, smells, or other signs that someone was there.

The hair on the nape of my neck stood up. Someone *was* watching me.

My heart began to race, and I snapped my head in the direction of a sudden noise, searching for the culprit.

CHAPTER TWELVE

I didn't see anything out of place, but my blood swirled with a sensation I couldn't quite understand. Even though my wolf didn't sense anything, I knew, without a doubt, that I was being watched.

Xander's hurried footsteps stopped behind me, and he stilled. He whispered so faintly only I could hear. "What's wrong?"

For half a second, I wished the two of us could pack-link, but then I remembered that would mean Ryker was my alpha.

Aw, *hell* no.

I'd rather be jumped than join a pack where I would be forced to do the alpha's bidding every time I disagreed with him.

"Something's in the woods," I muttered.

Xander came to my side and stared in the same direction. I knew what he was doing—using his wolf senses to see what I was talking about—so I wasn't surprised when he glanced at me and shook his head. "There's nothing there."

"Yes, there is." My legs began moving of their own

accord, even though my wolf whimpered inside me, agreeing with Xander that there was absolutely no reason I should believe anyone was there.

And yet, something inside me that I could only describe as awareness sparked. I couldn't get myself to stop heading toward the thicker trees, searching for answers.

"Dammit, Ember. Do you *want* to push Ryker over the edge? He's already livid, and your only saving grace is—"

"You act as if I'm not aware." Anger flashed through me. "Hell, 'livid' is probably an understatement for the rage and hatred he must be feeling toward me now." Still, I continued forward without hesitation.

"Then you know we should be heading back to the vehicle now. If they get back there before we do…"

I tuned him out as each step closer caused my heart to race. The most concerning problem was that I didn't know if it was from anticipation or dread.

A hand gripped my wrist, tugging me back and forcing me into a hard, muscular chest.

My blood boiled, and I spun around and punched Xander in the jaw. His head jerked to the side, and his eyes widened, but his grip didn't slacken.

"What the actual fuck?" he gritted out while narrowing his eyes. Even as his jaw turned red where I'd hit him, he didn't release his hold on me. Instead, he grabbed my other wrist too.

I growled, trying to wrench myself out of his grip, but he was too strong, and I was weak at the moment. I needed to recover quickly because I wouldn't be dominated by anyone…especially not men like them.

I did the only other thing I could think of—I spat on the ground, making my displeasure apparent. "I understand that your pack is callous and arrogant, but do *not* touch me like this again." My breath caught as the wind swirled through the branches, causing twigs to drop onto the mulchy ground. The air seemed to wrap around me like a blanket, warm and comforting despite the chill in the air.

He dropped his hands and took a step back. I exhaled. I hadn't expected him to release me that easily, especially when he'd just taken a blow to the jaw and I'd spat at him.

My awareness of the other presence vanished, leaving behind a faint coldness that reminded me of the way Briar's link felt.

It didn't make any sense. Something had to be wrong.

The wind eased, and the woods became eerily silent. My wolf's agitation churned uneasily inside me and urged me in the same direction now that the weird sensation had disappeared.

I took a deep breath, searching for any signs of a presence, but I heard only faint howling in the distance—Ryker and the others hunting down Simon.

"What the hell was that?" Xander muttered, stepping up to my side. His wrinkled forehead and the strained skin around his eyes screamed that something was wrong. He scanned the area I'd felt tugged toward.

A knot formed in my stomach. "What do you mean?"

"Did you not feel that gust of power?" His eyes glowed as his wolf surged forward, using its magic. "The wind wasn't natural."

I bit my bottom lip. "Are you sure?" It had felt natural to me.

"I'm positive." He lifted his chin, and his nostrils flared, but he didn't look away from the spot. "Why don't you head back to the SUV? I'll investigate before the trail gets cold."

I gritted my teeth so hard that my jaw popped. "We would already have been over there searching if you hadn't stopped me in the first place." If I hadn't wanted to conserve my energy, I'd have punched the jackass again on pure principle.

He cut his eyes at me and bared his teeth; however, I didn't wait for him to say anything else and moved quietly in the direction of the sensation once again.

"I said head back to the SUV," he called. "Not run in the direction of the threat."

A snort lodged in my throat as I increased my pace. I swallowed my laughter only because I didn't want to risk alerting anyone we were heading in that direction if they were still there. Just because I didn't sense them anymore didn't mean they weren't hiding. If they could control the wind, they could probably manage to do other things as well, but what supernatural species could even control the wind? The closest I could come up with was witches, but even then, the ability to manipulate air was rare and limited. No one was meant to truly control the elements of Mother Nature.

Still, the fact that Xander expected me to obey him made me want to laugh all over again. He didn't have any say over me even if I'd agreed to stick with them for now.

"Dammit," Xander grumbled loud enough for me to hear. "Ryker is going to kill me." Then his pace quickened to catch up.

I moved faster, risking making noise. Even though Xander seemed like a decent guy, especially compared to Ryker, he was still part of their pack and might try to prevent me from continuing on.

I focused on the woods. I could hear the sounds of deer, raccoons, and owls as they prepared for winter, indicating they didn't sense a threat. But Xander hadn't sensed the threat either at first, and when he had sensed magic, I hadn't, so who knew what we were up against or if the animals could feel the presence of the observer?

I stepped through the thickening brush, and a faint floral scent I couldn't place hit my nose. It smelled of sunshine and crisp tea leaves with a hint of mint and made a dull ache form deep within my chest, close to where my pack bonds used to be.

My feet stilled, and I glanced around. There was no sign that anyone had been there beyond the fleeting scent that seemed to dissipate quicker than should be possible.

Xander hurried into the area but stopped when our gazes connected. I held my breath, ready for him to insult me or try to drag me from this spot, but instead, his shoulders slumped slightly as if seeing me had given him some relief. Then he tore his gaze from mine and surveyed the area.

Good. I didn't want to waste energy fighting him.

Turning away, I took in the thick brush at the base of three sizable oak trees. They formed a *V* with the brush laid out like a thick, prickly blanket—a perfect place for hiding.

I tapped into my wolf, borrowing a little bit of her magic to enhance my night vision and hearing. Though I could see beyond the trees and hear the sound of some deer rutting, nothing seemed out of the ordinary except for the very faint smell...and the sound of paw pads hitting the mulch and heading in our direction.

My heart dropped to my stomach. Ryker would arrive soon.

"There's no way anyone was here." Xander took a deep breath and scowled.

"Well, that weird, alluring scent proves otherwise, though it's almost gone now." I didn't know how he could overlook that fact.

His brows rose so high it was almost comical. "What are you talking about?"

I leaned back on my heels. Why would he pretend he didn't smell anything odd? "The scent in the air. Something *was* here, though it doesn't smell like any supernatural species or human I know of." The words were out before I realized how they sounded. That was the thing... Scents didn't lie, and I didn't know what that meant for what I'd smelled.

He pursed his lips. "What are you talking about? There's no abnormal scent here."

I opened my mouth to argue but closed it. He was right. I couldn't smell anything anymore. Was my mind playing tricks on me? I'd been on the brink of death, separated from my sister, and trying not to mourn the slaughter of my entire pack. That didn't include the fact that I'd just used the bulk of my energy to fight Ryker, but no... Xander had sensed something too...something I hadn't.

Crossing my arms, I tilted my head. "You said you sensed magic when I didn't. We can't both be wrong." Surely not, right? Although...there was absolutely nothing to prove we hadn't both lost our minds.

"I..." He grimaced. "I don't know. None of this makes any sense."

For once, we could agree on something. I ran a hand through my hair, my fingers snagging in the tangles. I could only imagine what I looked like, but that was an entirely superficial problem.

I could make out Ryker's, Gage's, and Kendric's distant footfalls now. They were less than a mile from us and running at top speed, which meant they'd be here in a minute.

Xander closed his eyes for a second. "We'd better head

to the vehicle. Ryker is almost here, and he wants the two of us away from this spot so you can't cause any more problems while they search the area."

The familiar heat of anger flowed through me once again, a sensation I'd rarely felt and had never enjoyed prior to Reid's rejection. Now, it seemed to be the emotion most comfortable to me and helped me focus on anything but my pain. "Well, he wasn't here and didn't experience what we did, so I think we should be the ones searching, not them."

"Look, you're exhausted, and I could easily pick you up and carry you away if needed." He rubbed his jaw where I'd hit him. "And that punch you delivered caught me off guard. It won't happen again. Can you *please* do me a favor and not fight me on this? I'm fucking exhausted too, and I don't want to deal with Ryker when he's even more pissed."

He wasn't demanding but rather taking the extra time to talk to me like a person. I understood that we were all exhausted, and unfortunately, I had to admit that maybe I wasn't up for being part of the search, especially since I might have imagined everything. "Fine, but if they lock in on a scent, I want to come back and see the evidence myself."

"You always have to push him, don't you?" Xander sighed, and then his eyes glowed. After a few seconds, they returned to their normal color, and he nodded in the direction of the car. "Let's go. Ryker said *okay*."

My back straightened. I hadn't expected him to give in to my request so easily. Maybe he was desperate to get me out of the way.

Hearing how close the three of them were to us now, I headed back to the vehicle. Truth be told, I didn't want to be around Ryker any more than I had to. The more time we spent together, the more I didn't like the way he handled things.

Xander stayed close by my side, glancing back every few seconds like he was hoping that evidence would suddenly materialize to prove that the two of us hadn't lost our minds.

I kept my gaze forward. A part of me wanted to be wrong because, if I wasn't, that meant another species existed that I knew nothing about. A shiver ran down my spine, and the coldness settled in my chest in the form of another emotion I was beginning to feel all too often and wanted to channel into rage to burn it away.

Fear.

Soon, the woods began to thin, and the moon rose high in the night sky. Owls hooted in the distance, and the Suburban appeared in the darkness. My legs immediately dragged, exhaustion crashing over me. I didn't have the energy to crawl inside, so I leaned against the side of the vehicle and sank down to the asphalt of the parking lot.

Xander came to my side, and I expected him to open the door and tell me to climb in, but instead, he lowered himself to the ground next to me, and the two of us sat in silence.

The weight of the world pressed in on me. I didn't know how long we sat there, but as I got more comfortable sitting beside him, my emotions came on stronger. Comfort wasn't helping me hold myself together. The dam inside me was near to breaking, and pain, anger, and heartache crushed my chest.

Footsteps stomped in our direction.

Ryker.

He came into view, his eyes dark with anger as he pointed right at me. "You're going to pay for this."

CHAPTER THIRTEEN

E ven as anger flamed through my body, exhaustion had taken root, making it impossible to stand on my own two feet. Despite my annoyance, I couldn't order myself to get off the ground. Instead, I crossed my arms and scowled, hoping that I didn't look constipated. "Because losing my pack wasn't payment enough?" My voice cracked, making me sound weak and pathetic, but I didn't care. I hadn't done a damn thing to justify him talking to me that way.

The luster in his eyes lessened for a moment before it reappeared so heavy that I could barely see the actual color of his irises.

He stalked in our direction, a few twigs sticking out of his hair. The moonlight glistened on his shirtless body, and my traitorous eyes focused on the contours of his muscles and stalled on his chiseled six-pack. A different kind of warmth spread through my body, one I refused to acknowledge. Instead, I forced my eyes upward toward his face, which was way too handsome for the cruel person he was.

"Don't pull that card on me." He jabbed a finger at me. "We lost our pack too. You aren't the only victim."

A bitter laugh shredded my raw throat. "Oh, you're making sure there are plenty of victims." Adrenaline finally pumped through me, allowing me to climb slowly to my feet.

Xander lightly tugged my arm, trying to get me to sit back down.

"Do *not* touch her," Ryker snarled, his eyes glowing even behind the thick sheen. His hands clenched as Kendric and Gage hurried into view behind him.

Kendric's forehead creased, and he blinked with what had to be surprise while Gage's eyes widened and he lifted both hands.

"Okay, damn!" Xander dropped his hand. "I was just trying to help."

Baring his teeth, Ryker's chest heaved even more than before. "She doesn't need your help. Got it?"

In fairness, I agreed. I could handle my own damn problems just fine, but I didn't like that Ryker had made the determination for me. "If he wants to help me, then that's between him and me. You don't get to make that decision."

Ryker's hateful gaze landed squarely on me, and he rasped, "Maybe I don't make the decision for you, but I can and will influence *his* choices if he doesn't agree with me."

A sour taste filled my mouth. Alphas like him were the worst. They didn't hesitate to cut down a person or compel them to obey their commands. All the powerful packs, including the late king's, had a way of making sure they got their way, and it was one reason that my pack had been more reclusive than most. We'd kept our heads down so that we could live our lives on our own terms as much as possible. That had worked well for centuries—until several days ago.

He smirked and tilted his head in mockery. "What's

wrong? Upset that you can't get your way? What are you going to do? Punch me again? The first time, you surprised me, but believe me, lil rebel, I will tame you like I did the rest of them."

Lil rebel?

How ironic. All I'd ever wanted was to live in peace. Even now, I just wanted to find my sister and run away to where our enemies couldn't find us. A fresh start somewhere to build a brand-new life that wasn't haunted by the ghosts of the pack we'd lost.

Still, I refused to let anyone break me. I might want to live in peace, but that didn't mean I'd allow myself to be terrorized or broken by a bully. "I will *never* submit to you."

He arched a brow as if I'd offered a challenge. He rubbed his hands together and said, "You know what? I should make you submit to me and join the pack. That way, you won't free a fucking vampire who has answers and then pretend to sense a threat in the woods to get us to stop searching for him."

I flinched. I knew he'd be pissed at me for what I'd done back at the river, but I hadn't considered the possibility he'd think I made up the story of someone watching us from the woods. "It wasn't made up."

"See, I find it strange that you specified the incident as *it*." He cracked his knuckles while staring straight into my soul. "You could be referring to *anything,* and worse, you think I'm dumb enough to fall for that."

I huffed and eliminated the five-foot gap between us. My feet moved way too willingly—like I *wanted* to be close to him instead of my real reason—proving I wasn't afraid of him. But this was one of my pack's downfalls and another reason we'd stayed pretty isolated—we refused to cower when faced with someone like *him*. I refused to stroke his ego just because he was such a strong alpha. "I felt a presence back there, watching us," I whispered. I'd meant to sound sure, but maybe I'd imagined it after all. I was exhausted, injured, and constantly felt as if something might jump out and try to kill me.

Ryker sniffed and narrowed his eyes. "There's no hint of a lie, but you didn't say it like you were confident. I find it convenient that you fought me to let our best lead escape, and when we finally picked up his trail, we were suddenly called away."

I shook my head. "That's not what happened at all. I thought I sensed someone watching me."

"You *thought*?" Ryker leaned forward.

Kendric's and Gage's expressions were strained as they watched Ryker and me. They slowly flanked Ryker, their gazes darting back and forth like they weren't sure what to do or what was going to happen.

In fairness, I wasn't sure either, but Ryker infuriated me more than anyone in this world ever had before. His mere presence irked me, and I didn't like what that said about me. However, someone had to stand up for what was right in this world, or Ryker would make it his own version of hell.

Ryker cleared his throat. "Any day now, or are you choosing not to answer for a reason?"

I jerked my attention back to him. "I was certain until —" I cringed, hating that I couldn't finish my sentence. When Ryker grinned and clasped his hands together, I forced the rest of the words out. "I wasn't."

His mocking grin disappeared into a stern expression. "What does that even mean? There was no one there, Rebel. We sniffed out everything."

This was where I'd sound crazy, but I'd own up to my

mistakes. "I don't know how to describe it, but I *knew* someone was watching Xander and me."

"I'm going to need you to *try* to describe it," Ryker bit out.

Xander grunted behind me like he was standing up and might interject, so I didn't wait to start talking. "Awareness prickled inside me." I steeled my expression, though a part of me wanted to cover my face in shame. I was a wolf shifter, and my wolf magic had never sensed anything out of the ordinary before. I had no legitimate reason to think that someone was there...and yet, I had.

The stress, loss, and chaos must be getting to me. I couldn't even rely on my animal.

"What do you mean by that? Did your wolf sense something?" Ryker pressed his lips into a hard line.

If I said yes, my wolf would look weak, and I'd smell of a lie, so I had no choice but to come clean. "No, she didn't. My wolf didn't sense anything."

"So you used whatever you made up in your head as a reason for us to stop chasing that fucking vampire." He flushed, and a faint growl reverberated from his chest.

Xander stepped to my side and puffed out his chest. "Man, a gust of wind came out of nowhere. It freaked me out too, so it wasn't just her."

"Had she told you that she *sensed* something by then?" Ryker asked.

"Yeah, but—"

Ryker's nose wrinkled as he cut in, "You let her manipulate you instead of relying on your senses."

As if Fate agreed with Ryker, a breeze suddenly picked up like it had earlier, causing branches to rustle and more orange, red, and yellow leaves to fall to the ground.

"Do you sense something now as well?" Ryker snapped,

staring Xander and me down. "Or since Rebel hasn't said anything, does it just feel like fall weather in the mountains?"

The urge to punch him again built in my chest. I hated how condescending he was, and I couldn't help comparing him to the alpha I'd known best who would never treat a pack member or someone else that way. Yes, Dad would've been disappointed in me for letting my imagination run wild, but he also would've known that putting more pressure on me wouldn't help. I'd seen how he handled families that suffered a loss and weren't quite themselves for a time. He would have forced me to sit out from scout duty until things got better. Granted, I'd never done anything like what had happened tonight, but I'd lost my entire pack except for one person, and she was likely with an enemy I needed to find as soon as possible.

"I didn't make it up on purpose, okay? Besides, I had no way of communicating with you all to know that you'd picked up his trail when I felt the alarm." A small part of me screamed that I hadn't made up anything at all, but the logical side of me understood what extreme loss could do to a person. "I seriously thought I felt someone. There wasn't anything extra to it. You tracking down Simon was coincidental."

Gage patted Ryker's shoulder. "If she were lying, we'd know. Remember how we were for days, if not weeks, after our pack died? We were all on edge, thinking we were going to be attacked at any second. Hell, some of us still act like that."

At Gage's admission, my body felt a little lighter. Maybe I wasn't crazy after all. Lately, I'd felt like I was falling apart more each day instead of getting better. Could that be why I resented Ryker so much? I feared that

I would become like him and lose who I was in the process?

Cutting his eyes at his friend, Ryker scowled. "I know she's not lying, but that doesn't mean that ever since I found her near death, she hasn't been a huge pain in my ass."

I huffed, crossing my arms. "If by pain in your ass, you mean that I wasn't okay with you—"

"Do *not* say beating up a victim." He took two large steps toward me, getting in my face.

Immediately, the other three guys moved in, arms raised as if they were ready to intervene.

But I didn't need their protection. I could take care of myself, or I'd go down trying. I couldn't rely on anyone but myself. "Why? Because you might feel a little bit of remorse for what you did?" A little bubble of hope expanded in my chest. I suddenly *needed* to hear him admit to being a somewhat decent person, though I wasn't sure why.

"Because Simon's not a good being. That's why." He moved quickly, placing a hand on my arm.

The other three guys jerked forward but pulled back when they noticed his gesture.

The sheen dissipated from his eyes, allowing me to see warm brown with flecks resembling gold. My wolf fidgeted awkwardly as I got lost in those beautiful eyes. Between that and the tingles from his touch spreading through my body, I had to remind my heart to harden as I stepped back and squared my shoulders. I couldn't allow anything to distract me from my hatred of him. I had one task, and it was way more important than any draw to a man—especially someone who could turn on me at any second.

"Why should I trust you? You've given me absolutely no reason to, and your pack's reputation speaks for itself. Do you even know Simon?"

And just like that, the sheen settled back over his gorgeous irises, and the strange sensations in my stomach calmed. Good. I didn't need any more confusion. I'd found a self-destructive path well enough on my own.

"I don't need to know him to know he's no good." He dropped his hand and snarled. "And if you're going to question my judgment, then maybe you should *go*."

My heart lurched. Finding Briar on my own might be more difficult.

Taking a deep breath, I found my resolve. "You're right. Maybe I should go on my own. Your antics are distracting me from finding Briar and our real enemies anyway." We'd wasted time chasing down innocents instead of the real threat, and it probably would be more effective to search on my own.

Gage snorted, his stern expression vanishing, until Ryker whipped his head in his direction and growled.

Gage lifted both hands, and his expression sobered though his eyes held a hint of sparkle. "What? She just called your ass out. It's sorta refreshing. No one has done it since—"

"Do *not* speak her name," Ryker bit out in a voice part human and part animal, suggesting he was on the verge of shifting.

Xander gripped my shoulders and tugged me back a few steps until my back pressed against the vehicle.

Ryker recoiled and focused on me as fur sprouted from his arms. "Do *not* touch her. I've already told you once." He was on the verge of losing control.

"You're about to shift, and I was getting her out of the way." Xander once again dropped his hands like he'd touched something hot. "What the hell is wrong with you? You're acting even angrier than usual."

Ryker's chest heaved. "Because nothing's gone the way it's supposed to ever since *she* joined us. We should be getting answers, but instead, we're searching for fictitious supernaturals that she *felt*."

What a control freak! The fact that I had my own mind infuriated him. "You know what? You're right. I'm hindering you, and you're hindering me. Let's just cut ties and go our separate ways." I needed to follow the pack link to Briar and stop wasting time fighting with him and torturing a vampire who'd just lost a ton of people he must have cared about.

Ryker lifted his chin, and at this point, I couldn't even see his eyes through the sheen. "Fine. Go," he said condescendingly.

I spun on my heel, hating that he'd given me permission before I made the move on my own. I would now have to figure out on my own how to save my sister from whatever pack clearly had it out for us. Still, it was better to get there and figure it out instead of wasting precious time hunting down innocent people in hopes of quicker answers.

I marched past Xander and around the back of the vehicle. Since we were in the area where I'd grown up, I could easily avoid the wolf territory lines and stay close to town. Half the Shadowbrook population was human, so it wasn't deemed any supernatural's official territory.

I'd just reached the main road so as not to stray into Asher pack territory when I heard footsteps hurrying behind me.

"Ember, wait," Ryker rasped.

I spun around, and when I saw the way he stood before me, I stopped in my tracks.

CHAPTER FOURTEEN

He hung his head, and his shoulders slumped, making him appear almost like a different person. He kicked the ground, causing a few pebbles to scatter to the side of the road and ping against the trunk of an oak tree.

I hated that I'd turned around. I should've just kept going. Nothing good could come of a conversation between the two of us, but the damage was done. Seeing him less confident tugged at my heart at a time when I needed it to remain impermeable. "Want to insult me some more?" I sneered.

"No." He shook his head. "You don't need to go after your sister alone, and I don't want you to leave our pack."

I snorted. His regretful tone didn't make sense. He'd been a dick ever since he pulled me from the water, and the only reason I'd been biting my tongue as much as I had was because he *had* saved me from drowning. "I have a hard time believing that. You were going to leave me on the side of the river without any help. If not for your pack members, I might have wound up dead."

He flinched then exhaled and lifted his head so our eyes met. "You're right, but I'm trying to find the real enemy and didn't want to be slowed down. It was one life at stake compared to thousands I've sworn to protect."

Inhaling sharply, I shook my head. "You were willing to let someone of your own species die when you've sworn to protect us? Do you realize how contradictory that sounds? If you start deciding whose lives matter and whose don't, you take on the role of Fate, which isn't our place in this world."

The luster appeared in front of his eyes once again. "I'm not asking for your opinion on how I handle things. I just realized when you walked away that maybe I was too hard on you."

"Too *hard* on me?" I parroted and clenched my jaw. Too hard was when you told someone they should've done better after they gave it their all. This...this was just cruel. "Why don't we call it what it is? You're a control-freak jackass. I feel horrible for your pack because you have no problem with alpha-willing them, and the fact that you can't control me drives you crazy."

"It does." He sighed, the sheen flickering in and out of focus. "Because I'm not used to being disobeyed, especially when I'm doing things for specific reasons."

"If you had reasons for tormenting Simon, *please* share them with me. Explain to me why I was wrong." I crossed my arms, daring him to. Even though I hated to admit it, I wanted to know why he was so convinced that torturing Simon was the right call. I wanted it to be more than just him having no problem inflicting pain on someone else.

"As much as I would love to explain everything to my pack and to you, I can't." He shook his head and straightened his shoulders. "So you're just going to have to trust me."

"*Trust* you?" He couldn't be serious. All my life, I'd heard stories about the way the Grimstone pack was run and the viciousness they practiced in the name of protecting the royals, and since meeting him, I'd found he lacked so many morals that I valued in a person and leader. "You've done *nothing* to deserve my trust. In fact, everything you've done has made me see how you toe the line of doing just enough that the wolf shifters don't want to get involved...for now." If he tried torturing an innocent wolf shifter or even a witch with pack ties, our species *would* get involved, and it would not go well.

He winced, the golden flecks of his eyes warming the brown color. "It's all to discover who slaughtered the royals and our packs, Ember. Don't you see that?"

"No, I don't. But even if I did, is the cost of losing who you are as a person worth it?" My heart quickened as if his answer was important to me.

His forehead furrowed, but then the strange sheen slid firmly over his irises once more. "Yes, because they'll continue to slaughter us at will, and I'm the protector of our species. I don't take pleasure in torture, but the burden lies squarely on my shoulders now, and I'm doing what has to be done." His words sounded emotionless and fit the arrogant alpha I'd come to know.

I rolled my eyes as my anger spiked. What sort of narcissistic asshole thought they knew best and could protect the whole world all on their own? A dictator, that's who. And that's exactly what he'd become to his own pack. "You must think awfully highly of yourself to take on protecting our entire species, especially after being unable to protect the royals and your own pack." I slapped a hand over my mouth, surprised by my own words. I hadn't even processed what I was about to say, and now I'd sounded almost as cruel as he was.

His eyes darkened once again to where I couldn't see the color anymore. The little bit of the person his pack members had told me about vanished, and I swallowed. However, this version of Ryker I understood, and seeing him helped me remember all the reasons I should never be around him.

"I think I'm not the only one changing after suffering a loss like that." He arched a brow and sneered. "Because, based on your reaction, the old Ember wouldn't have said anything like that."

My face heated, and I hated how accurately he'd just called me out. In fairness, I'd just done the same thing to him. I deserved it. "I'm sorry. I shouldn't have—"

"Don't apologize to me. You meant it." He crossed his arms and tilted his head. "You just hate that you spoke the words out loud to me. See, that's the difference between only thinking it and having the guts to say it."

I straightened my shoulders. "What I think in one moment doesn't mean it's my truth, and sometimes, it's better not to say something without thinking through the consequences."

"Maybe in normal times, but *Rebel*, we're at war. We don't have time to cater to people's *feelings*. If we waste time like that, then our enemies will find us, and we'll be dead."

He'd completely missed my point, and my hands itched to strangle him. "It's not necessarily only feelings that would be impacted." I jabbed my finger in the direction of the woods. "You just tortured someone who witnessed an entire nest get destroyed. Someone who might've been willing to talk if you hadn't started drowning him, especially since we all understand what he'd just gone through."

Groaning, Ryker rubbed a hand down his face. "Get over the fucking vampire. You're investing way too much time in him."

With hurried steps, I moved within a few feet of him. "That's my point. Who's going to want to help you when word gets out that you have no issues tormenting someone?"

"First off, he was a vampire. No wolf shifter or witch is going to care." Ryker dropped his hands, his expression sharpening. "And second, I don't care if you don't agree with my strategy. My decisions are my own, and I do what I believe is necessary. I followed you to ask you to come back, so are you coming back with me or not?"

Wow. We didn't know each other well, and what we did know of each other drove each of us insane, but he'd come after me remorseful then changed back into the jackass I'd been determined to get away from. I'd known better than to stop to talk to him. Damn my traitorous legs. "And why would I do that? You were the one who basically told me to leave just now. Good job pretending to be sorry for a few minutes. You did enough to get me to listen to you. Until *now*." I *hated* that I'd been so foolish. I still didn't understand why I'd even stopped.

Ready to fix that problem, I pivoted to get back to getting the hell out of here.

Feet shuffled behind me, and a massive hand caught my wrist and tugged me back around.

His scent filled my nose, making me dizzy and further pissing me off.

"Look, I get it, okay?" he said through clenched teeth. "You're not happy with me. If we focus more on following your pack link while trying to find answers, will you stay?"

I jerked away from him, my skin colder where he'd

touched me. "Yes, because going about things your way hasn't worked. Look at where it's gotten us."

His eyes narrowed. "If you hadn't—"

"Freed a vampire who we hadn't seen do anything wrong from being beaten, you'd have gotten everything you needed," I snapped, cutting him off. This was the entire point. He still wasn't sorry, but his pack must have influenced him to try to get me to stay. At least they seemed like decent people. In fact, I felt bad for them. Not only were they dealing with the loss of their pack, but they were also forced to do things against their will.

Throwing my hands up, I took several steps back, needing distance from him. "We keep having the *same* conversation, so let's just cut ties and be done. Let the other three know you tried to get me to come back, but the differences between us are too great. I refuse to lose more of myself by being around you."

He blinked hard and growled. "Fine. I'll try to abstain from doing anything you would disapprove of this strongly."

"Why? Why would you do that if you're so adamant that you're doing what's right?" I must be missing something...something that would explain— Cold realization drenched me, and I realized that I had control over this. I'd bet his pack members hadn't told him to rush after me after all. He hadn't expected me to walk. He'd thought I'd stand down because I didn't want to be alone.

"Because it's not right, you being alone when they could be targeting you." He rubbed his hands together. "You can't defend yourself and—"

"You have no leads." I crossed my arms, victory soaring within me. He had *nothing* to go off of, and the enemy hadn't attacked him and his pack again despite their not being quiet about where they were. However, I might be a different story, especially if they had my sister. "And you're hoping they're using my sister to track me. My pack link is the only thing you have in your favor to locate them." I refused to be played. Maybe my wolf wasn't as strong as his, but I wasn't dumb or weak. "You need me more than I need you."

Face reddening, he laughed, but it sounded strained. "That's a bit extreme. There are four of us and one of you."

"But I have something to go off of." It would work, too. It would just take longer than someone handing over the information.

"Are you coming back with us or not?" He scowled.

"On one condition. It's nonnegotiable. No more torturing or hurting someone who hasn't done anything to deserve it." Even though I didn't like it, I did understand that there could be times when torture might be necessary, but this incident with Simon was different. In a perfect world, we'd imprison or exile wolf shifters who'd done something awful, but that wouldn't fix this problem. There had to be a pack out there, if not multiple ones, working together. We had to defend ourselves, no matter the costs.

He grimaced. "I will have..."

I rocked back on my feet, waiting for him to tell me there was no way in hell he'd agree to that. But the color of his irises brightened, and I thought I could see his true self once more.

"I'll struggle with that, but I'm willing to oblige you as long as you focus on finding your sister." He cleared his throat and kicked at the ground.

Air swooshed into my lungs, and my brows arched. "Did you just agree to my condition?" That was the last thing I'd expected him to do.

"Yes, I did." A vein in his neck ticced like it pained him to admit that.

Part of me wanted to gloat and make this a huge deal, but we didn't have time to waste. It was petty and wouldn't accomplish anything except taking longer to locate my sister.

I needed to focus on our pack bond. My heart sank. I knew that by doing this, I would have to acknowledge the one hundred and three missing links. I couldn't deny that not wanting to face the loss head-on had allowed me to go along with Ryker's plan. Anything was better than allowing the grief to dig in.

Maybe him asking me to come back wasn't a great thing after all.

"Having second thoughts?" He arched a brow, the flecks of his irises warming.

There was no way I'd admit weakness to him. "Let's go back and get this going." I couldn't lie to him without him knowing, but I also didn't want to let him see my concern.

He pressed his lips together like he was stopping himself from saying something. Instead, he nodded.

Without another word, I walked back toward the group, Ryker by my side.

The eerie feeling of being watched surged through me again. A shiver ran down my spine, but I forced my eyes to keep looking forward. I wouldn't let my mind distract me again.

Within a minute, Ryker and I joined the others. Kendric was pacing in front of the other two while Gage leaned on the vehicle and Xander sat on the hood. The three of them watched us approach.

"I knew you'd get her back." Gage beamed and winked. "We haven't had this much fun in a long while."

Fun? I wanted to laugh, but the urge died in my throat. I was fighting with Ryker about everything he and I did. We were at complete odds. "I'm not sure you could call it that."

A cell phone dinged, and Ryker removed one from his back pocket. He looked at the screen and frowned. "Holy shit. This isn't good."

CHAPTER FIFTEEN

I leaned over and read the screen.

All Pack Alphas in the immediate area are to meet to discuss the future leadership of the packs. This Friday 7 PM at the Local Wolf Bar in Shadowbrook.

My stomach dropped as realization sank in. Now that everyone thought my entire family line had died, they weren't wasting any time trying to name a new ruler and royal pack bloodline. We were the only ones with even the slightest hint of royal blood who hadn't been part of the royal pack, and I was sure several of the alphas would now believe they should be the ones to lead the shifters.

My heart clenched, thinking about all that implied. "This is horrible timing."

"What's going on?" Kendric crossed his arms, placing his hands under his armpits.

"The Blackwood pack just called a meeting of all available alphas." Ryker bit his bottom lip like he was trying not to say more.

Xander straightened. "That's fucked up. Calling that meeting is supposed to be *your* role."

Technically, that was true. The hierarchy for our species was based first on royal blood and then on the strongest pack who'd served as their protectors, which meant I was the most directly in line to rule because of my blood, and Ryker was the next because he was the strongest wolf since he was the protector, even though something like this had never occurred before.

"Are you really surprised?" Gage pushed off the side of the vehicle and wrinkled his nose. "Every pack out there *hates* us. They think we either failed to protect everyone and shouldn't lead or were behind the massacre, but there's no way to prove it. Of course, several of the alphas want to be the new *king*."

And, of course, my *fated mate*'s pack was the one to send out the message. Reid had made it clear he'd hoped that, once we were mated, he and I would step up to rule since my dad wouldn't. Killing my pack put him in a position to accomplish that without me.

My stomach roiled, and I wanted to vomit. I'd already shown enough weakness around them, so I swallowed it and let the acid burn my throat.

"That must be why he went after your pack," Ryker growled, echoing the thoughts I'd just had. "I suspected his pack might be behind all this. They're one of the closest to where we lived, and between what they did to your pack and now this, the signs point to them."

Even though Reid had rejected me and I'd witnessed the start of my pack's slaughter with my own eyes, something about the situation still felt wrong. After decades of our packs having a strong relationship, it was hard for me to reconcile that they'd do that to us.

The idea of having to walk into the bar and see Reid again had my knees weakening. Everything he'd done to me had made me feel weaker than ever before, which infuriated me. And now he'd called a meeting that would influence who would lead our species. It made me want to strangle him with my bare hands.

The violence of the urge strangled *me*, making me feel like another person...a dark version of myself who turned my blood to ice.

Dad wouldn't have wanted that. If he knew my thoughts right now, I'd be so ashamed. Taking a deep breath, I placed a hand on my stomach. "That doesn't make sense. Assume you're right, and Briar is with them; her pack link would be a lot warmer than it is now. She has to be farther away than that." Her link was still faint—just enough for me to know she was alive.

"If they suspect you survived, then they'll probably take her far enough away that you two can't communicate and confirm anything." Kendric rolled his shoulders like he was trying to work out stress.

"Yeah, because seeing the Blackwood pack attack her own wouldn't raise any red flags." Gage snorted bitterly and shook his head.

True, but that didn't seem like it was the plan. "I'm pretty sure Briar and I were supposed to die alongside them. Reid knows how close my sister and I are. He's keeping her alive because he knows I'm still out here and I'll come for her." A lump formed in my throat. I hated that I couldn't get a sense of Briar's health or what was going on with her. She could be near death, and I'd have no clue.

"This would be an ideal time to examine his land—the Blackwood alpha family is focused on the meeting." Xander rubbed his hands together. "Maybe we can finally get a lead without having to torture anyone."

Ryker scowled. "No. Not happening. That could be part of their plan, knowing Ember could be tempted to check out their territory while they conduct the meeting. They could eliminate her as a threat to the throne and be seen as the pack stepping up to lead. We can't risk walking into a trap."

My heart dropped hard into my stomach. I hadn't even considered that which proved that coming back with Ryker, though not ideal, was the better choice. He'd grown up strategizing, whereas my pack had stayed away from politics, wanting to live in peace without the negativity so many packs had.

Maybe if Dad had also allowed us to study warfare, I would've seen the signs that Reid wasn't a nice guy.

"So what do we do?" Gage spat, disgust apparent on his face. "Just hide and let him conduct the meeting?"

I didn't want to hide, but I wasn't sure what else to do. I needed to keep my head down so I could find Briar before time ran out.

"Nope. We do what no one expects." Ryker steepled his hands in front of him. "Rebel will embrace her nickname and show up with me at the meeting."

My jaw dropped. "I don't think that's a smart idea."

"But it is." Ryker's gaze landed on me and warmed once more as he grinned. "Because that is the last thing any of them would expect. It will throw the Blackwoods off-kilter if you show up when they're trying to claim there's no one of royal lineage alive any longer and see that you aren't afraid of making a stand."

Bile churned in my stomach. Unfortunately, he was right. They wouldn't expect that, but that didn't mean I wanted to go and confront the people who'd killed my pack.

My eyes burned with the threat of tears. I bit the inside of my cheek, focusing on the sharp pain of my teeth sinking through the skin.

"He's right." Xander pursed his lips. "You'll ruin the Blackwoods' plans, which could make them act rashly and reveal where your sister is being kept."

Even though that was true, I hated to give them what they might want—me, dead. Still, if I didn't show up or search their lands, they might think Briar was lying and I *was* dead. Either choice had consequences.

I wished Dad was alive so he could guide me on the right thing to do. My heart ached, stealing my breath. The pain of losing both parents and almost my entire pack took hold. I feared if I didn't push the pain away, it would take me down, and I'd lose Briar in the process.

For some reason, my gaze landed on Kendric, who was rocking back and forth on his feet. He stared at the moon as if he were in deep thought.

"Imagine those fuckers' faces when you stroll in." Gage laughed. "That would be the last thing they expect."

My attention flew from Kendric to Gage, whose eyes shone with mirth. He did have a point. If I were going to die, at least I'd have the victory of making Reid uncomfortable one last time. That had to count for something. Still, before I agreed, I asked Kendric, "What do you think?"

Of the four, he was the quietest and seemed to have a different perspective. He'd mourned the loss of the vampires like they weren't the species we got along with least.

Kendric's brows shot up, and he cleared his throat. "I agree with the others. Showing up makes the most strategic sense." He cut his eyes to Ryker as they darkened with disapproval.

Not flinching, Ryker either didn't notice or didn't care. He lifted both hands. "So it's up to you, Rebel. You going to be a pain in their ass too, and not just mine?"

I laughed, the sound raking up my throat and startling me. I had to agree, out of all my options, that would be the one everyone would expect least. Maybe they'd make a mistake when rattled. "Fine, but it's not for two days. I don't want to pause our search for Briar until then."

"We can still follow your pack link if you can figure out which direction to take." Ryker placed a hand on his chest. "I'm all about confronting them and proving those assholes did it sooner rather than later, so if we can do that before the meeting, I'm in."

For the first time, Ryker and I seemed to be on the same page. My stomach fluttered, though I couldn't figure out why.

I didn't want to analyze it. "Then I agree."

He smirked, and my feet inched a little toward him before I stopped myself.

"We need to get going." Kendric gestured to the vehicle. "We have to deal with what happened to the vampires. We've already wasted too much time."

The little bit of kindness that had appeared on Ryker's face vanished. I wondered if it was a figment of my imagination.

"You're right." Ryker ran a hand through his hair, and a few pieces fell over his forehead. "Let's head out."

The tingle that warned me someone was watching us grew stronger, and I glanced over my shoulder in the direction the sensation was coming from. Just like last time, nothing was there.

"Are you feeling that pull again?" Xander asked, coming to my side and staring in that direction.

I shook my head, realizing that the sensation came after strong emotions. Why was I allowing my mind to mess with me? "It's nothing." I dug my fingernails into my palms, determined not to delay us. The guys were ready to leave, which meant we could rest and begin searching for Briar sooner.

Still, the sensation seemed to grow stronger—like it wanted me to listen to it.

"We've already wasted enough time here." Ryker slashed his hand through the air. "There's no one there."

I gritted my teeth, my wolf not liking how he'd spoken to us. Still, arguing with him was futile and would only make me look worse. Like last time, there was no reason to believe someone was there. We would have heard them, smelled them, or sensed *something* tangible for them to get this close.

With every ounce of self-control I had, I ordered myself to turn my back and walk away.

Gage opened the car door for me, bowing ever so slightly as I climbed in, and this time, he got in the back, switching spots with Kendric.

I climbed into the very back, the strange sensation dissipating. I still couldn't stop myself from glancing out the side window in the direction it had come from.

Within a minute, everyone was loaded, and Ryker scanned the area one last time.

A flash of light caught my eye, but as soon as I blinked, it had disappeared. "Did anyone see that?" I rasped.

"What?" Xander turned in my direction, worry lining his forehead.

"A flash of light." I had to be freaking him out, but I couldn't do a damn thing about it. I was scaring my own damn self too.

"There was nothing out there." Ryker glanced in the rearview mirror as he turned the vehicle around. "I checked before pulling out."

What the hell was wrong with me? Was I losing my mind because I was sort of a rogue wolf right now, with Briar being so far away, or was this a phantom sensation from the pain of losing my pack, my wolf wanting to feel a connection to someone?

Gage's head popped around his headrest, his lips pressed into a line. "Maybe you should get some rest. You've had an awful few days, and going through what you just did affected all of us in different ways."

I hated feeling weak, but he was right. I wasn't back to full health, and I had *just* lost almost everyone. Maybe the stress had somehow disconnected my human and wolf sides and they were both trying to survive, which was making me feel weird things. There were so many possibilities I wasn't sure of the cause. Maybe it was a combination of everything.

The four of them glanced at me periodically, making me feel as if I were under a microscope, so I did the one thing that made the most sense to me at the time.

I lay in the back seat and closed my eyes, trying to block out the world. I needed rest...a break from the pain, stress, and demands that my body and mind kept making.

Before I realized it, I drifted off to sleep.

"Just because they wanted us to come here doesn't mean that we should have," Ryker said tersely. "I hate giving them the illusion of control over us."

"Man, you know it's not like that," Kendric grumbled. "When I told Raven everything, she said it would be best if we came here and talked to them in person. Besides, it's a free place to stay for a few nights, and we're low on funds."

I tried to open my heavy eyelids but struggled. I wanted more sleep, but the conversation I was hearing had me concerned.

"What are they going to say about *her*?" Xander whispered, and I guessed he was talking about me.

Gage sighed. "Who knows, but we're about to find out. I still think we should've woken her to let her know where we were heading. It's not right."

They *were* talking about me. My eyes flew open, and I sat up. Then my entire world froze.

Fuck no. This had to be some sort of nightmare. There was no good reason for the four of them to have brought me *here*.

CHAPTER SIXTEEN

I blinked several times, hoping that my mind was once again playing tricks on me. However, I recognized the oaks of the forest I'd run by so many times, and then Ryker took a turn down the dirt road that led to the place shifters were forbidden to go unless invited by the vampire royal.

Each time I tried opening my mouth, no words would form and soon, the royal vampire house on the outskirts of Shadowbrook towered before me.

Even though I'd never seen it before, rumors of the opulence of this house had spread throughout the supernatural world because of the splendor but also because of the way it was guarded. The queen was over a thousand years old—one of the oldest rulers in vampire history—and wards had been placed around her estate by witches who'd owed her favors during the nine hundred fifty years she'd reigned.

The essence of magic pulsed past my skin, and an iridescent sheen seemed to roll over the lawn, faintly lighting up the dark night. Together, it enhanced the Victorian sensibility of the stone mansion that stood in front of us. Dark green slanted roofs jutted above each window of the top floor, faint golden light peeking through thin white curtains.

A matching stone driveway seemed to go on for miles until it circled in front of a square porch with stairs leading up to an arched entryway. A dark stone statue of a gorgeous woman with long flowing hair towered in the center of the circular drive...and I suspected that it was of the queen herself. Even in stone, she was stunning.

No one but the royal wolf-shifter pack had ever ventured here, and even then, it was only once a year for the centuries-old tradition that kept the peace between wolf shifters and vampires. Something that had been established about three hundred years ago by the queen herself and one of the strongest shifter alphas who had ever lived, though the disdain and mistrust between our two species had never truly gone away.

My stomach dropped. I'd be surrounded by vampires. Though not as strong as wolves, they were fast, and here we were *greatly* outnumbered.

"What the fuck are we doing here?" Had the vampire queen learned what they'd done to Simon and somehow forced Ryker to bring us here? "And why didn't you wake me up before pulling up to the fucking front door?"

"Wow. I don't think I've heard you cuss that much the entire time we've been around you." Gage's head popped up in the middle-row opening. His expression was relaxed, like nothing was amiss. "And here I didn't think I could like you any more than I already did, you little spitfire."

Ryker slammed the car in park and snarled, "Shut up, Gage, before I make you."

Of all the things to be upset about, Ryker was focused on Gage?

Kendric glanced over his shoulder. "There's nothing to worry about. We aren't in danger."

My mouth dropped open. Was I experiencing some demented nightmare? "We're surrounded by vampires!" What they'd done to Simon must have been haunting me for me to have a messed-up dream like this one. The fact that I clearly felt guilty and thought I should be punished alongside them, despite me being the one who freed him, spoke volumes.

"I told you we should've woken her up sooner." Xander crossed his arms and frowned. "If I were her, I'd be upset as well."

At least *he* understood, but the fact that he didn't seem upset about it himself made the world spin around me. "If someone doesn't explain what the hell we're doing here, I may actually lose my damn mind." I pinched the inside of my wrist, hoping that would shock me out of whatever sort of hell we were in and pronto. Sharp pain radiated from my wrist, but I remained sitting in the car in front of the vampire queen's house. Awake.

I never should've agreed to rejoin these idiots. I should've gone with my gut and left them behind despite Ryker's appeal.

"There's no need to be alarmed." Ryker sighed.

I could see him roll his eyes in the rearview mirror.

"No need to be alarmed?" I parroted back, my heartbeat quickening and my wolf stirring. "Look at where you've brought us. Did the vampire queen learn about Simon? Were we summoned? Is that why we're here?" That was one of the rules established between vampires and shifters. If any sort of atrocious act of violence was committed against one species by the other, the royals of each species could summon the leaders and those accused of the crimes.

To date, that had never occurred, mostly because the conflicts were intraspecies fights or disagreements, but we had tortured one of their own after two houses full of vampires had been slaughtered. If *atrocious* needed a definition, I could get behind that one.

"We weren't summoned." Kendric's eyes warmed. "We came here to inform them of what we found at the two houses."

I blinked several times, my brain glitching. "Why not just call?" Even though I could get behind transparency, especially if we were fighting against the same enemy, we didn't need to show up at the door and hand ourselves over. What if they learned what had happened with Simon?

"Because something like this should be communicated in person." Kendric hung his head.

Before I could ask, the front door of the mansion opened, and a breathtaking woman came out. Her dark hair streamed behind her as she ran barefoot to the vehicle.

"Here we go. I'm not looking forward to telling her all the details and how we found Adira," Kendric muttered and then opened his car door.

When the woman ran straight into his arms, my head jerked back, but that was nothing compared to the way my lungs seized when I watched Kendric wrap his arms tenderly around her. The gestures were intimate—but they weren't of the same species.

Chuckling, Gage shook his head. "I told you not to worry. I understand your concern and discomfort, but after the deaths of the royals, the vampire queen reached out and offered us assistance and a place to stay. They've treated us better than any of the wolf shifters have, and we've grown close to many of them."

I rubbed the back of my neck, needing to do *something*

with my hands. Even though I understood his words, the combination of them didn't make sense. I exhaled, trying to gather my wits and calm my racing heart. "That's why the vampires called you for help." Now that didn't seem so random and strange.

"Unlike the wolf shifters our pack protected for centuries, the vampires opened their homes to shelter and protect us when we were abandoned by our own kind." Ryker's jaw worked, his muscles constricting.

"Maybe if your pack wasn't known for being so cutthroat and the four of you hadn't run off so suddenly beforehand, the other packs wouldn't be so suspicious of you." I didn't like most other packs, but the sudden deaths of the royals and Ryker's father had placed Ryker one step from the throne. The fact that he hadn't tried to take it left everyone even more on edge, wondering what he was planning. That was one reason the other packs had pressured Dad or me to ascend. We had the bloodline claim that Ryker didn't.

Ryker became a statue, and a chill ran down my spine. When Gage and Xander both grimaced and all the warmth they'd emanated toward me vanished, my heart seemed to stop. I'd just insulted the four people who were supposed to help me find my sister.

But they had to be held accountable for their actions.

"We *didn't* run—we were called away to a nearby vampire attack," Ryker snapped, and then he shoved open his door and got out.

Xander shook his head, his disapproval cutting worse than Ryker's, and followed his alpha's lead, leaving me in the vehicle with Gage.

A knot of shame sat heavy in my stomach, and I tried to push the sensation away. I kept my eyes forward, waiting for

Gage to voice his displeasure and climb out, but all he did was sit there, staring at me.

After a few seconds, I couldn't take it any longer. "Just say what you want and go out with the others. I plan on sleeping in here tonight." There was no way I'd enter a nest full of Fate knew how many vampires. These guys might trust them and have an understanding, but I did not.

"Ember, I know you're struggling. Hell, we all are." Gage cleared his throat and placed a hand on my knee before continuing, "But a lot of people could claim that you ran when your pack was being killed too. Don't you think it's a little hypocritical to be tossing around the same accusation that could be used against you?"

His words were worse than a punch to the gut. The pain was so sharp and intense that I even wrapped my arms around my waist, trying to minimize the pain. I hadn't considered that some would claim I ran for self-preservation. I'd acted to protect my sister and obey my father, but I had no way to prove that beyond my own word. "I—"

"Don't." Gage shook his head and smiled sadly. "I think you've said enough for now. You've never asked us for our version of our story, and I get why. Not only would you be forcing us to relive our personal hell, but you'd be reliving your own as well. Yet, with the attacks escalating, I don't think any of us can afford the luxury of ignoring those days. At least, not until we locate your sister and defeat our enemies. You do realize that we all need to work together to accomplish that, right?"

My face flamed—he was completely right, and I was allowing my emotions to get in my way. I'd never had that problem before, but Ryker somehow brought out in me all the anger and frustration I never even realized I had. It was a very hard lesson to learn. "I...I can't trust you four. The last person I thought would protect me shamed me in front of everyone and might have slaughtered my family." The sting of rejection flared inside me along with the words Reid had said—*There's something wrong with her*.

Gage chuckled, the sparkle that I'd already grown accustomed to returning to his irises. "Don't worry, sweetheart. Ryker doesn't trust you at all either, but you did agree to an alliance with us. We're not asking for anything beyond that...yet. And even then, it could just be an added bonus of pleasuring one another." He winked and scanned me from head to toe, making his intentions clear.

Even though Gage was one of the sexiest men I'd encountered, and I could use a distraction, nothing sparked between us.

Strange.

All I could assume was that it had something to do with Reid being my fated mate, which meant I might never be attracted to another person as long as I lived. At least I'd had a few partners before I became celibate.

This night kept getting better and better.

"As nice as that sounds, I'm going to pass." I tried to smile, but I had no doubt my strained expression made it fall flat.

A hand pounded against the glass, startling me.

Gage exhaled and leaned back. "It's time to tell the vampires what happened. Raven is falling apart, knowing that none of the vampires are answering her calls. They sent a group of their guards there to check things out, and the queen is demanding an update."

Lovely. I could only imagine how our story was going to sound, especially after they learned about Simon. I could only hope and pray that they'd believe Ryker and the others when they said we weren't behind the attack. "Do we have to go inside to speak to her? What if it doesn't go well?" I had no clue why the hell we'd risked coming here, knowing that one nest had been slaughtered and we were the last ones there.

"Yes, but she's not here," Gage reassured me.

My brows furrowed. "What do you mean?"

"This is her primary residence, but she has several other houses where she spends time." He lowered his voice. "All of them are near the Blue Ridge Mountain range because she wants to be where the majority of the shifters and about half the witches live. She also has houses in several of the cities in the area, including here, Asheville, and Charlottesville, Virginia, plus a location that no one outside her closest circle knows the whereabouts of. Raven told Kendric earlier that Queen Ambrosia left two days ago, heading to Asheville for some sort of celebration."

A weight lifted from my shoulders, and my lungs worked freely once more. But I didn't want to get my hopes up. We were surrounded by vampires and at their mercy. "Still, they—"

"Raven was the one who asked us to go." Gage squeezed my leg. "They know we aren't the ones who attacked the vampires. They just want an update."

I swallowed and inhaled. There was no stench of a lie. He truly believed it, which did help, but what if he was wrong? Either way, it didn't matter now. I was already here and surrounded. It wasn't as if I could leave. Ryker and the others wouldn't let me, even if the vampires wouldn't stop me.

Gage's eyes glowed, and there was another round of pounding on the door. I leaned forward as Ryker shoved Xander out of the way, his eyes a bright yellow from how hard his wolf was surging forward. He yanked open the door and snarled, "Get the fuck out of the car."

"What the—" Gage exclaimed, but when his head snapped in Ryker's direction, his voice cut off. "Damn, okay. I was just talking to her for a moment. She was freaked out!" He climbed out of the car, and Ryker jumped into the seat, taking his place.

His gaze met mine, and my wolf responded.

A deep growl came from his chest, and I lifted my chin in defiance.

CHAPTER SEVENTEEN

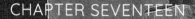

I had no clue what I'd done to piss him off this time, but I wouldn't jump out of the car like Gage just because Ryker glared at me. I straightened my shoulders, ready for the inevitable argument about what I'd done wrong.

When he opened his mouth, I cringed, preparing for an insult or snide comment.

"I'm sor—" His eyes flicked down toward the floorboard.

The last bit was so muffled that even my shifter ears couldn't pick it up, but if I didn't know any better, I would've thought that he just apologized to me. "What?"

He closed his eyes and groaned like I'd punched him in the balls. "You're not going to make this easy for me, are you?" He looked at me, the color of his irises vivid to the point that I could see each speck of gold hidden within the brown.

My wolf stirred even more inside me, but I ignored her, focusing on the man in front of me. "I'm honestly not sure what you said." I must have misunderstood him.

He cleared his throat and ran a hand through his hair. "I'm sorry," he whispered, just loud enough for me to hear.

A lump formed in my throat, and my stomach fluttered. "For what?" I needed to get my head out of my ass because this would be where he cut me down with his words.

"For not waking you and informing you of what we planned." He sighed, and his shoulders dropped. "If I were you, I'd be pissed if I woke up in vampire territory."

All the anger that had been boiling inside me cooled, which wasn't what I wanted. But how could I stay mad at someone who'd apologized and admitted they were wrong? I still wanted to tell him where to go, but instead, something different left my mouth. "You probably didn't even think about it since you all clearly trust them."

My eyes widened at my words. But it was true—with everything else going on, he probably hadn't considered how I'd feel.

"I—er—*we* didn't." He licked his lips and dropped his hand back into his lap. "But I should've. After we provide Queen Ambrosia with an update, if you aren't comfortable staying here, we can leave. We did gather our supplies from the last place we stayed—where we located you in the woods—since Simon could track us down, but we can rent another location if needed."

How long had I been out? I glanced up at the descending moon. It had to be close to two in the morning. I'd been out for at least five hours...and I still felt tired. "Did you all really stay here after..." I trailed off, unable to speak the words. I didn't have to because, from the way his eyes darkened, he understood.

He sighed. "Yes, for about two weeks while we acclimated to our new reality and what the other shifter packs thought of us. Queen Ambrosia arrived at our lands while we were burying the d-dead." His voice broke on the last word. "She offered us a place of safety until we could get back on our feet. We couldn't stay there, and the wolf shifters who stopped by scorned us, so we accepted the offer, and I'm glad we did. They've been the only support we've had."

I had no argument for that. I'd rather stay with a coven of witches I knew nothing about than with vampires. At least witches had natural magic like us, magic from the earth. Vampires' magic came from draining life instead of fostering it. Our two magics were completely at odds. Vampires were fast but not nearly as strong as wolves. We could see them with our wolf vision; even when they moved so fast they blurred, and we had the strength they lacked. "Couldn't you have provided an update over the phone, especially after what happened with Simon?" I didn't doubt that the news about Simon would make the queen and the other vampires angry at us. They'd be loyal to their own species over wolves.

"If I was worried about that, then we wouldn't be here." He winked.

My stupid heart skipped a beat.

What the *hell* was wrong with me? The nice, sexy shifter who'd flirted with me didn't faze me at all, but one second of kindness from Ryker and my heart was doing all the crazy things. Was it because my wolf knew that Ryker and I were nothing to each other and my future with my fated mate wouldn't be impacted by him?

I needed to make myself feel something for someone I could have a future with and get over this fated-mate bond crap. Reid had betrayed me and my entire pack and might be holding my sister hostage.

I shook my head, trying to get my thoughts back on track. "Why wouldn't you be worried about that? He's a vampire, and we're at the queen's mansion. If she learns what we did—"

The hard edges returned to his expression. "I'm telling you—Simon isn't who you think he is. It will be fine."

"You—" I started, but Ryker opened the door and jumped out.

When Ryker extended a hand toward me, I shut my mouth and crossed my arms, tempted to refuse to get out of the vehicle.

"Rebel, I need you to trust me." His expression softened, and there was an urgency in his stare as he continued to hold out his hand toward me, asking me to take it...to have faith in him.

Xander, Kendric, Raven, and Gage stood there, watching us, along with a group of four vampires who'd stepped out of the front door.

The last thing I wanted to do was insult the vampires. They could kill me with no repercussions if they chose. I was on their lands, after all, and had been involved in the torture of one of their species.

I forced myself to climb through the middle row. Without meaning to, I took his hand, and a buzz hummed between us. I gasped as the golden flecks of his eyes seemed to sync with the faint electricity that flowed between us.

All of a sudden, that sheen covered his irises once more, and the pleasant sensation vanished, leaving my hand in his warm, tight grasp.

My knees almost gave out, but I managed to keep moving without missing another beat. I needed to let go of his hand and fast; before something else strange happened between us. *What the hell is wrong with me?*

It had to be effects from the loss of my pack and being cut off from my sister. I was basically rogue.

Raven sniffled and stepped between Kendric and Xander so that she stood in front of me. A tear trailed down her cheek, but she smiled and placed a hand on my shoulder. "I promise you'll be safe here. You have my word. Anyone the Grimstone pack brings to the mansion is welcome at any time, per Queen Ambrosia's orders."

"Really, babe? It's not because you trust us?" Kendric teased gently, hooking an arm around her waist.

The easy, romantic affection between them caused my spine to straighten, and I hated that my heart flared with jealousy over it.

Reid and I were supposed to have something like they did.

She rolled her eyes and wiped the stray tear away. "Of course I do, but the queen's decision has a bigger impact than my own."

Even though I could tell she was trying to tease, her eyes looked haunted, and I suspected it had nothing to do with her being a vampire. "I'm sorry for your loss." I felt something tugging at me, making me want to comfort her.

She pressed her crimson lips together and squeezed my shoulder comfortingly. "Thank you. One of the vampires there was a close friend of mine, so forgive me for being overly emotional. From what I hear, I should be saying the same to you as well. All of us here have lost so many people important to us."

The lack of sulfur and the way her bottom lip trembled made me realize that she did, in fact, understand my pain. Adira must have been the friend and why Kendric had been so upset to tell her the details. A sob built in my chest, but I'd be damned if I cried now. Not in front of Ryker and a bunch of bloodthirsty vampires.

She dropped her hand and took a step back like she

could sense my turmoil. "Come inside; the queen has been waiting for an official update. You can give it to her chief guard." She spun around, taking Kendric's hand in hers, and the two of them headed to the door where the four vampires were waiting.

Ryker stepped to my side while Gage flanked the other, and when my gaze drifted to the left and right of the house where the oak trees thickened, I realized why. About ten guards were watching us from afar, five on each side.

I swallowed and muttered so softly that only the two of them and Xander could hear me, "I thought you said we were safe here." With the way they'd surrounded me, I wasn't quite sure anymore.

"We are, but we need to make sure you don't do anything rash and change their minds about allowing you to stay here with us," Ryker replied as he took my hand and looped it through his arm.

Thankfully, there were no strange sensations this time, but I still resented the way my hand naturally curved into his arm like I wasn't revolted by him. He wasn't someone I'd ever like; he'd tormented an innocent vampire, alpha-willed his pack members into submission, and Fate knew what else.

The way the vampires stared at me made my skin crawl —granted, that was likely their intention. Instead of cowering, I lifted my head and looked straight ahead, pretending their attention didn't affect me.

Strangely, Ryker's touch seemed to calm my turmoil enough that I could pull my act together.

Three men and a young woman stood by the door. They all had similar brown skin, eyes of varying shades of green, and dark, tight, curly hair that many people would die for. The young woman was about five foot two, about half a foot shorter than me. The other men were like stairsteps, with the youngest-looking being the tallest of the three.

The woman lowered her head at our approach and lifted the edge of her long dress to curtsey. "I didn't realize we had an extra visitor—the four of us will prepare another room for her."

My stomach dropped, thinking about being alone in a room with a house full of vampires. The words sounded like the punchline to a joke at a shifter bar.

"No need." Ryker slipped his arm around my waist and pulled me into him. "She'll be sharing a room with us."

Even though the last thing I wanted was my body pressed against his, I despised that I didn't hate the feel of it. In fact, my heartbeat quickened a little too much. I took a deep breath, trying to control my reaction. If this was what it took to stay with the four of them, so be it. I'd feel safer with them than anywhere else here, a fact which spoke volumes.

"As you wish." The woman clasped her hands together. "We'll have cooked meat ready for you after the meeting."

The four of them spun around and hurried into the house, leaving the door wide open.

We entered a gigantic foyer with a staircase that twisted to the second floor and a massive window showcasing the mountains behind the mansion. A table to the left was decorated with four lamps and a Gothic black cross that towered in the middle.

Raven turned right and led us through an archway into a massive office almost the size of my entire house.

The interior walls were made of stone, and there was a huge television in the center of the wall directly across from the entrance. A colossal dark cherry table sat in the center in front of it, and three vampires stood at the other end, each holding a cup filled with a dark-red liquid.

The coppery smell of blood hit my nose, informing me exactly what the liquid was.

My stomach rumbled, and Gage stepped closer to me, probably sensing my discomfort. I tried to keep my legs steady as Raven nodded to the two women and the man, who wore an all-black suit.

The taller woman's russet-brown eyes focused on me, and her forehead creased. The shorter blonde woman tilted her head. The man pursed his lips and said, "Why is there another wolf shifter here?"

The hairs on the back of my neck rose in warning as my wolf eased forward.

"She came with us," Ryker rasped.

Xander and Kendric angled themselves in front of me as if the vampires were preparing to attack us.

"The queen didn't mention another shifter being allowed here." The brown-eyed woman wrinkled her nose and removed a dagger from a sheath at her side. "Only the Grimstone pack is allowed here, and she isn't part of it."

"Calm down." Raven laughed a little too loudly. "I informed the guards at the gate that they could let her through."

The blonde, who appeared to be in her thirties, snarled, "You may have more power than most, but not even you have that authority, Raven. She needs to leave, or we'll make her. She doesn't have permission to be here. If we'd been alerted—"

"If she leaves, so do we." Ryker laced his voice with alpha will, though it wouldn't make the vampires submit to him. Still, their heads jerked back, proving they could feel the power he possessed. "And we won't give your *queen* an update."

Animosity hung thick in the room, making it hard to breathe. Clearly, not all the vampires liked us being here.

"Are you sure you want to make an enemy of Queen Ambrosia?" the blonde woman spat, setting her glass on the table. "Because I've been dying to sink my fangs into you and rip out your throat."

Letting me go, Ryker inched in front of me in a protective stance. "Just make the first move so I can defend myself."

"Gladly." The blonde laughed then blurred toward us.

CHAPTER EIGHTEEN

The Grimstone boys moved together, blocking me from the blonde vampire. I gritted my teeth, not liking that they believed they had to protect me. My wolf inched forward, fueling my body with some of her strength since we didn't have time to shift.

My legs moved quicker than ever before, and I sprang forward, shoving my way between Ryker and Gage just as the blonde vampire reached us. She seemed to move at quick human speed instead of vampire, and she now held her dagger in her hands, utilizing her momentum to swipe the blade toward Ryker.

No!

I punched her in the jaw just as a commanding voice shouted, "Stop!"

The blonde's head jerked as she stumbled several steps back and slashed air with her blade.

A gasp sounded behind me, and the reality of what I'd just done began to sink in. But if I hadn't, Ryker would've been injured, if not killed. Still, I'd never moved that quickly before...

"What in the *world* is going on?" the voice demanded, causing all the vampires except the blonde to freeze and cast their gazes at the television.

My ears rang, and my pulse thudded in my neck.

It had to be the vampire queen.

Still, I couldn't take my eyes off the blonde vampire, who straightened and bared her teeth at me just as blood trickled from the side of her mouth. She could attack again at any second, and this time, she'd make sure I was her sole target.

Ryker wrapped one muscular arm around my waist and pulled me against his chest. His hard muscles pressed into my back for a moment before he pivoted to stand in front of me.

I stepped to his side, preventing him from trying to protect me again.

"The Grimstones brought a stranger here without getting permission first, and Raven took it upon herself to allow her in without clearing it with *us*," the blonde gritted out as red seeped through her emerald irises, revealing that her vampire instinct was taking over.

"Which she didn't have to do," the voice from the television snapped. "I told Raven that when it comes to our wolf-shifter friends, she makes the final decision."

The floor seemed to tilt under my feet. I hadn't expected the queen to take Raven's side. Everyone knew that the head guards were the ones the royals relied on to know what was safe and not.

The blonde's attention snapped to the screen, and her fangs descended. "Your Majesty, I thought we agreed that from here out—"

"That was your first mistake, Lucinda," the woman interjected. "*We* don't need to agree on anything. I told you that I usually trust your judgment. That doesn't mean I suddenly approve of you making all the decisions when it comes to our wolf-shifter *friends*."

The tingle of warning in my spine ebbed to the point that I felt comfortable enough to redirect my full attention to the screen.

The most gorgeous woman I'd ever seen sat on a red velvet and gold throne. Her long chestnut hair waved past her shoulders, and her maroon lace dress had a slit from her breasts to her belly button that revealed the curves of her cleavage.

A knot formed in my stomach, and while I personally had never been attracted to a female, for the first time ever, I understood why others might be.

"Your Majesty, you know better than to trust *them*." The blonde's jaw clenched as she pointed her dagger in our direction like she had to be clear on whom she was referring to. "The last time—"

"That is *enough*." Queen Ambrosia straightened, her gray eyes narrowing. "Do I need to remind you of your place in my court? I'd hate to have to put you, Martin, and Bella through all that again." She bit her plump, pink bottom lip and arched a perfectly sculpted brow.

"That won't be necessary." The guard, who must be Bella, shook her head vehemently. "We just didn't realize that someone outside the Grimstone pack was allowed to enter without being vetted by us."

"Especially one who can move faster than any shifter I've seen before." Martin wrinkled his nose and side-eyed me. "Let's not pretend no one noticed."

This was another reason that our pack had stayed off the grid as much as possible. For some reason, wolves of my lineage could move faster than usual, especially Dad when he thought we were in danger or when we were hunting something hard to catch.

Chest tightening, I cracked my neck, trying to think of a way to salvage the situation. "Adrenaline spike is all." That was what Dad had always claimed.

"Kendric alerted me that they'd taken in someone who'd suffered a similar fate as they had... and as we did tonight," Raven explained, moving to stand on my other side. "She was also with them at the nest houses, trying to protect our people from the attackers. There was no reason to believe she was a threat and every reason to think that she could provide more insight, especially about the details surrounding the attack on her pack."

"Her pack?" Queen Ambrosia tilted her head as her gaze landed on me. "Are you from the Sinclair pack?"

I opened my mouth to lie but paused. I was used to being around witches who didn't have a sensitive nose. Vampires, however, could smell a lie, just like the wolf shifters. "I am."

"*Really*?" Her eyes widened, and the corners of her mouth tipped downward. "I heard there were no survivors. How were you able to escape?" Compassion filled her eyes as she brought a dainty hand to her chest.

"I...I really don't know." That was true. Between the weird things and strange emotions and sensations I'd been experiencing, I wasn't sure what was legitimate and not. But Briar had been petrified and had run too—I hadn't been alone. "All of a sudden, my pack links began disappearing. When we ran out to help, chaos erupted. The Blackwood pack was attacking us without any warning."

Shaking her head, the queen dropped her hand and leaned forward. "The Blackwoods did this?"

I nodded, and my stomach churned. "But that doesn't

make sense. And someone chased my sister and me, but I never made out who it was." For some reason, I couldn't bring myself to say the words. This damn fated-mate bond was becoming a real pain in the ass, preventing me from speaking ill of Reid despite what I'd seen with my own two eyes.

Ryker laughed bitterly. "Even after the alpha heir insulted you and rejected you in front of hundreds of shifters, you're still trying to protect him?"

My face heated, and I wanted to hang my head in shame. He was right. I sounded and looked pathetic. Maybe there was something wrong with me after all, but that didn't matter. I had to find Briar.

Queen Ambrosia twitched. "Wait. Are you the Sinclair alpha's firstborn?"

The question knocked the air from my lungs. The threat of tears burned in my eyes. "Yes." Even though, technically, that wasn't true anymore. Dad was gone, which made me the actual Sinclair alpha. "At least I *was*."

"Did you arrive while the attack was happening?" Raven asked, turning her attention to Kendric. "Because you never said anything."

Kendric lifted a hand. "No. We did go by their territory a few days later, but we didn't know about the attack until we found *her*."

"The shifters didn't alert you?" Lucinda slid her dagger back into its sheath. "What good is it for us to have an ally who isn't kept informed by their own *kind*?"

Queen Ambrosia's entire body stilled to the point she didn't even seem to move in order to breathe. Her gray irises filled with crimson, giving her a dangerous edge. "You've made your displeasure about *my* decision known. One more word of disagreement, and I'll ensure that the only job you're offered is scrubbing the toilets. Do you understand?"

Hands clenched at her side, Lucinda rasped, "Yes, Your Majesty."

"I suspect I wasn't informed because Blackwood is making a move to take over the shifter throne." Ryker tugged on his tight black shirt, which already hugged his muscles. "He just texted a message to local shifter alphas, requesting a meeting in three days' time. If I hadn't found Ember near death in the river, I'd have shown up at the meeting uninformed and ill-advised. He's setting me up to make it appear as if I don't have the knowledge or influence to lead the shifters."

Cold realization settled into my bones. I hadn't even considered the ramifications of Reid's plans. I just assumed he hadn't informed Ryker because he didn't have his number, but Ryker's explanation made more sense, especially since Reid had been able to notify Ryker of the meeting that would be happening soon.

"That's one thing I appreciate about vampires." The queen tossed her hair over her shoulder. "They're content with what they have, and I don't have a bunch of people vying to kill me and take over my position."

Raven clasped her hands. "That's because we all love and respect you, my queen." Her voice trembled with affection.

"And I cherish each one of you, sweet child." The queen smiled fondly and took a deep breath. "Which is why I need to move the conversation along. Even though I hate what happened and feel for Ember, I want to hear about what you found at the vampire nest in the city."

"When we arrived, only one vampire remained alive

and was on the brink of death." Gage took in a shaky breath. "She wasn't able to provide us any information."

"Did you not find a single attacker there?" Queen Ambrosia crossed her legs. "What scents and signs of struggle were there?"

Ryker launched into the story, detailing everything we'd seen and experienced. "There was a faint smell of shifter that vanished within minutes."

"It must have been the Blackwoods, using the witch affiliated with their pack to mask their scents." Bella moved to the wooden chair at the end of the table and sat. "We can't stand idly and not respond."

Vampires blatantly attacking a pack would cause a war between the species, which might be exactly what the Blackwoods were going for, but still not ideal overall.

"That's probably what the Blackwoods want." Xander rolled his eyes. "You'll make them look like the victims."

Martin wrinkled his nose the way I would if I smelled something foul. "The redhead saw the Blackwoods attack her pack. She can tell everyone we were defending ourselves."

I laughed before I could stop myself. The queen and everyone in the room stared at me.

"Of course a shifter doesn't want to protect vampires," Lucinda sneered. "How *surprising*."

"That's not it." I'd never imagined I could hate someone I'd just met in so little time, but I would gladly rip out this bitch's throat given the opportunity. "The day before the Blackwoods attacked, Reid *rejected* me publicly. And if I were asked whether I saw one of them kill a member of my pack, I couldn't say yes because I never actually saw it happen since I was trying to protect my sister. I did see him lunge toward one of them. Plus, when we reached the vampire nest, I didn't recognize any particular scent that would have confirmed it was one of them. My word would do *nothing* for your case." A week ago, the details probably wouldn't have mattered, but today, they did. Reid had changed my world in the blink of an eye and in more ways than I'd ever thought possible.

"So neither of our *allies* are respected in their community. *Lovely.*" Martin scratched his sparse, gray-speckled beard.

The queen hit one hand against the velvet throne and dug her black nails into the material. "Our allies are some of the strongest in their community, and they *can* gain the respect needed when the time arrives. Are you questioning my judgment?"

"Of course not, my queen." Martin lowered his head. "I apologize if it came across that way."

Raven crossed her arms, glaring at the three guards. "You know how shifters are—the strongest always rise to the top. Respect is earned by the raw force of alpha magic."

"Besides, if the shifters go too long without a royal leader, their magic will begin to suffer, which means we need to take advantage of the upcoming meeting." Queen Ambrosia tapped her fingers along the new tears in the armrests.

A jolt shot through me. Even though Dad and my pack had known, the information was heavily guarded, withheld from most shifters for fear that someone would reveal it to the other species. We'd all wanted to keep the connection between our ruler—the strongest of all alphas—and our wolf magic a secret so the other species couldn't use it against us.

Clearly, the secrecy had been in vain because the vampire queen knew all about it and had thrown it out there carelessly.

Queen Ambrosia laughed. "The face each of the wolf shifters is making is hilarious. I've been alive for *centuries*. Do you really think I wouldn't have accumulated such knowledge in that time?"

That was a fair point, but still. I had a hard time fathoming why any knowledgeable wolf shifter would have informed the vampire queen of such information. "Of course not, but I'm a little confused as to why you'd want to help us instead of preventing someone from rising to rule."

Ryker's head snapped my way, and he frowned while Kendric, Xander, and Gage fidgeted in their spots.

She tilted her head and blinked, scanning me. "I appreciate your bluntness. Not many would dare to ask such a direct question."

Gage mashed his lips together, trying to hide either a scowl or a smile.

"Sometimes being direct is the best way to assess the situation." That was what Dad had always claimed. He'd believed that keeping political agendas hidden was counterproductive, whereas being direct and open-minded could help accomplish anything in this world.

"Fair enough." Queen Ambrosia leaned forward. "We don't want the wolf shifters to weaken. We agree with the witches' belief that all things must be in balance. If one type of magic weakens, then Fate will weaken us all."

I hadn't expected that answer. "Makes sense."

She smiled widely, her sharp canines on display. "I'm glad you approve. So what's the plan for this meeting?"

My breath caught as fear coursed through me even as I stared at her, dazed by her beauty. To shake myself out of it, I homed in on Ryker.

When I realized he wasn't staring at the screen

displaying the queen but instead watching me, I started breathing once more.

His face twisted into a smile far more breathtaking than the queen's as he replied, "Cause a scene and leave a lasting impression."

CHAPTER NINETEEN

"What the hell does that mean?" I gaped at Ryker.

I hadn't expected his smile to be so arresting. The queen's smile had *nothing* on his. A lump formed in my throat.

Why the hell was I noticing him so much? I needed to focus on what sort of plan he had up his sleeve.

His gaze stayed on me, and my heart lurched into my throat. If he'd been this stunning all along, I'd never have gotten a word out. My wolf inched forward, growling with approval.

Down, girl, I internally chastised, needing her not to add to my growing confusion.

"I already told you that we both need to attend the meeting, but it might be more fun to put the Blackwoods even more on edge." He winked, looking nothing like the angry, cynical alpha I'd come to know.

I opened my mouth to question him further, but no words formed.

"Man, come on." Gage snickered. "Tell us. Don't keep leaving us on a cliffhanger. Your dad pulled the same shit all the time. It has to be part of some alpha strategy training book the two of you read together or something."

Ryker snickered, rolling his eyes. "Well, if the Black-woods are behind this and they're trying this damn hard to discredit my pack by trying to set us up like we're the ones behind the attacks and desperately trying to kill all of yours, we should give them something to actually fear."

The thought of making Reid and his pack fear me brought the butterflies fluttering in my stomach to a halt. My entire focus was returned to locating Briar and getting even with my enemy. "Which is?"

"The two people they most fear winning control of the throne being together." He motioned to me and back at himself.

Now I felt like I was trying to solve a complex math problem. The answer was clearly in front of me but just out of my understanding. "Were we not arriving there together already?" I'd assumed we would be, seeing as I was staying with them.

Queen Ambrosia chuckled. "No, *child*. He means showing up together as *lovers*."

Instead of disgust, my damn heart skipped *another* beat. Nope, not happening. I wouldn't develop emotions for Ryker. Clearly, Fate wanted me to be attracted only to men who could destroy me as if the fated mate she'd chosen for me hadn't been cruel enough. Still, that didn't mean I would succumb to another one of her tortures. "I don't see how that would accomplish much more than just arriving in each other's company."

"But it would and might actually provide an advan-tage." Lucinda sat upright in her chair as the other two vampires flanked her. "Two of the people they fear most, allied and romantically linked. That will unnerve them and maybe cause them to do something reckless."

I bit the inside of my cheek so I didn't outwardly react, focusing on the sting I inflicted on myself rather than what these people were asking me to do. Yet, even that didn't push away the thoughts for long. They wanted me to not only face the man who'd rejected and publicly humiliated me but do it while pretending to be with a man everyone else hated. While making it seem like I hadn't only allied with him but taken him as a lover. The thought alone had my stomach churning. "I don't think we need to add the romantic element. I think showing up together will be enough. We don't need the extra layer."

Raven pursed her lips, scanning me.

A chill ran down my spine. Could she see more than I wanted?

"I know what we're asking is a lot, given how he's been acting lately," Gage said, placing a hand on my shoulder. "But having two people with the most legitimate claim to the throne united as a couple will make it even harder to ignore that they'd be stronger together."

I hated that he made sense. It would be hard to deny our claim, especially if we had an heir. Still, the thought of having to pretend to be attracted to Ryker didn't appall me, which was the biggest part of the problem.

A threatening growl came from Ryker on my other side, and suddenly Gage's eyes faintly glowed. The pack link was being utilized.

Dropping his hand, Gage stepped back and huffed abruptly. He placed his hands behind his back as if emphasizing that he wouldn't touch me again.

Strange.

"Fine." At the end of the day, there were two things that

mattered. "If you all believe it could help, I'm in. Anything to get Briar back before something happens to her."

"Briar?" Queen Ambrosia leaned back. "Who is that?"

I'd left out that part of the story, not wanting the vampires—especially the guards—to know that there was someone out there who meant everything to me. Enemies thrived on finding out people's weaknesses, and after losing my pack, I'd sacrifice anything for her. Still, the damage had been done after my speaking so carelessly. "My sister. I believe the Blackwoods have her and are keeping her hostage to try to locate me or get me to find her."

The queen frowned before she let out a faint gasp. "Oh, thank Fate. Not everyone in your pack perished after all." Her eyes glistened with what I thought must be unshed tears. "That's so lovely to hear."

I hadn't expected such heartfelt concern, especially from the queen of the vampires. "It would mean a lot more if I knew she was safe and unharmed."

"Then we must find her as quickly as possible." Queen Ambrosia took a slow breath and then turned to the vampire guards. "Give us your update and then give whatever resources are needed to Ryker and Ember to help locate Briar. It's imperative that we assist them so we can rest assured that the right wolf becomes the new ruler for the good of every species."

Now I understood how peace had been possible between our kinds. She cared about all supernaturals; otherwise, she wouldn't be able to empathize the way she was.

"We found nothing beyond what the wolf shifters stated —other than *their* scents," Bella spat, her face twisted in disgust. "So, either we're being played by the shifters or any clues about who attacked the nests vanished by the time we arrived. If it's the latter, then a witch must be involved."

Kendric bared his teeth. "We didn't attack your nests. How many more times are you going to accuse us of being your enemy?"

"Our spells would detect any scent-mitigating spells on them, so if there isn't sulfur in the air, they speak the truth." Queen Ambrosia shook her head and stood.

Martin pouted. "There's no scent of a lie nor any indication of magic on them that would hide the smell, Your Majesty."

Of course, she'd have spells in place to detect if we were trying to hide anything. She'd been around for centuries, enough time to collect favors from witches to do her bidding, especially since supernatural blood made coven magic much stronger when included in a spell or seance.

"Even though I trust the Grimstones, I do have detections in place in the event anyone tries to deceive us." Queen Ambrosia gestured to her guards. "That's one reason that I get annoyed but appreciate the fact that my guards are cynical because they're being protective of me and our species. It's why the three of them do their jobs as well as they do."

"We understand their mistrust regarding outsiders because our pack is the same way." Ryker spoke slowly like he was controlling his tone. "That's the only reason that we tolerate it. However, we came here alone, and we're completely outnumbered. That should provide reassurance that we don't want to risk our relationship with you."

Lucinda leaned back in her seat. "Unless you're trying to lower our guard."

She had a point, but I wouldn't admit it to the treacherous woman. Instead, I wrinkled my nose, wanting to convey exactly how I felt about her.

Mimicking my gesture, she made her point clear as well.

We despised each other.

"That's enough." The queen sighed. "My decision regarding the Grimstone pack stands. Please take them to their rooms and allow them to hunt in our woods for sustenance."

My stomach dropped. Even though I enjoyed being in wolf form, I preferred eating in human form. Unlike most shifters, I didn't enjoy killing prey, and I didn't eat as much meat, balancing it with fruits and sweets. I blamed it on my upbringing. All the shifters in my father's lineage had an affinity for sweets. Still, eating was eating, and I had to stay strong to locate and save Briar.

"As you wish." Raven smiled, taking Kendric's hand before continuing. "The quadruplets should have their room prepared by now."

That must be the four similar-looking vampires who'd greeted us.

"Good. I have business to attend to, so I must leave. If there are any issues, please alert me immediately. Lucinda, Bella, Martin, I'm counting on you to ensure the shifters remain unharmed and protected here while under our care. Do you understand?"

"Yes, Your Majesty." Martin's neck twitched as if it pained him to say the words.

Raven turned our way and rolled her eyes. "Now that we've settled all that, let's get you to your rooms so you can get something to eat. I don't smell a strong meat odor on any of you, which means you probably haven't eaten in a while."

I flinched, realizing it had been almost twenty-four hours since we'd eaten. No wonder I'd crashed so hard. Between needing to heal and not getting enough calories, I hadn't had the energy to accomplish it. I needed to rectify that.

We followed her into the hallway, leaving the other three vampires alone. I knew they'd be talking about us. I didn't like being somewhere that I wasn't wanted, but lately, that seemed to be wherever I went—including with Ryker and his packmates.

We headed back through the entryway, walking past the stairs and turning left once again. I glanced to the right and took in a formal dining room with a table that could easily seat twenty. Over it hung a grand chandelier in the shape of a skull, made with diamonds and red rubies placed in a way that resembled dripping blood.

A shiver raced down my spine. Ahead of me, a gigantic room with a glass wall that showcased the yard and woods came into view. Three large crimson couches sat in a *U* in front of a TV and splayed on them were three vampires, one on each couch, each having sex with a human as they drank from them.

I diverted my eyes to the TV and blushed. Some sort of porn was playing, which had my entire body flooding with embarrassment. I'd had sex before, but we didn't have sex openly like this and never with others in the same room.

Moans and sucking noises echoed in my ears as the strong scent of copper filled my nose. The urge to gag surfaced, but I swallowed, fighting the sensation. The last thing I needed to do was offend the very people who could decide to attack us at any moment.

Ryker slid an arm around my waist, pulling me to his chest so my vision was blocked, a welcome relief. The sounds were still bad enough.

Tingles spread from his touch, and I breathed in his scent, which seemed intoxicating. Need shot through me, catching me off guard. The fact that I was attracted to him was problematic, but this was taking it to a different level. It had to be the influence of the scene before us.

I stayed close, not wanting to embarrass myself further.

Soon the sounds and scents faded, and he loosened his grip on me.

Knowing I needed to break whatever hold he had over me, I took in a deep breath, allowing his scent to fill my lungs once more before lifting my head. We moved along to the kitchen, where the quadruplets were pouring blood into glass cups on the other side of a huge marble island.

The stench of copper hit my nose again, and a sour taste filled my mouth. The girl took a sip from her glass and then smiled, revealing pink-stained teeth and elongated canines. "Your room is ready."

Gritting my own teeth, I tried to keep a neutral expression, not wanting to reveal my disgust. I understood that blood was their sustenance, but the fact that it came from humans, who shifters and witches protected, upset my stomach. This was one reason that vampires and shifters were naturally at odds.

Ryker didn't hesitate, guiding me past the vampires toward the door at the far end.

My pulse pounded in my ears as we entered a massive, stone-walled bedroom. Two queen-size beds lay against each of the left and right walls, totaling four. Matching beige comforters on each had been folded down, showing brown sheets and pillowcases. Like the living room, the wall to the outside was all glass, including the sliding door cut into the center.

Turning to Kendric, Raven kissed him. When she pulled back, she said, "You five shift and go run and eat. It'll be morning soon, and you all need rest. This is your safe haven for as long as you need."

"We'll spend time together tomorrow, right?" Kendric arched a brow and cupped her cheek.

The gesture was so tender and intimate that my heart clenched hard once more. That was something I'd never have. But I'd rather survive with the pain and anger than be mated to Reid, who didn't have issues slaughtering my entire pack.

"Of course, but right now, I need to go speak with the guards." She pecked his cheek and then turned to me and continued, "And I want to get to know you a lot better tomorrow."

Her gaze was kind, but the hairs on the back of my neck rose in alarm. They did that whenever a vampire got too close because of their unnatural magic—a witch's spell gone wrong had made these immortal creatures.

I forced a smile and chose my answer carefully. "Okay." This was a trick my sister used on my parents. She wouldn't agree with them but, rather, would inform them she acknowledged their words.

She sashayed from the room, Kendric watching her every step, while Gage and Xander hurried to the sliding glass door. My wolf inched forward, bursting to get out, and my stomach rumbled.

Ryker led me forward once more, and as soon as we stepped through the door to the outside, Kendric's footsteps hurried to catch up.

Within seconds, we reached the woods, and I hurried to a sizable oak, where I removed my clothing. As soon as the chill hit my bare skin, my wolf surged forward, taking control. I tingled as fur sprouted, and my spine cracked until I was on all fours.

And then I was off, running to where Ryker and the other three were waiting for me.

The five of us ran through the woods, listening for signs of prey. The wind rippled through my fur, and my muscles burned.

The sounds of a herd of deer caught my attention. My head snapped toward the west. Saliva pooled and dripped down my jaw.

A few seconds later, Ryker and the others snapped their heads in the same direction, hearing the same thing I had. I couldn't pack-link with them, but I didn't have to right now. I knew what they were saying, *food*.

The four of them took off, the advantage of a pack link. I'd have to follow their lead and be a few seconds behind so I didn't mess up their attack and cost us a meal. I trailed them, though my wolf urged me to quicken the pace and take the lead.

Fighting the alpha urge even as it reared its head, I noticed their gait increasing. As Xander and Ryker separated to go around a tree, I saw the deer in front of me—four does and two fawns.

I'd scarcely paused to see which one the others selected before choosing my own when something dark appeared, barreling toward me and moving faster than anything I'd ever seen before.

Before I could adjust for the attack, something sharp pierced my shoulder and caused my leg to give out.

CHAPTER TWENTY

I whimpered, unable to hold in the sound, as my attacker pushed me onto my side. The faint, sweet scent of vampire mixed with the sweaty scent of human hit my senses.

Pawsteps stopped near me, followed by a low growl.

Wrenching my head to the side, I sank my teeth into my attacker's neck. Blood spilled into my mouth, the taste of cotton candy and copper making me gag. My jaws slackened as a man stumbled back, his fangs still elongated. He breathed rapidly, and his pale green eyes widened, showing a dotted outline of crimson.

I stood, unable to put weight on my left foreleg, as the sound of panicked breathing and quickened hoofbeats rang in my ears—the deer were fleeing.

On my three good legs, I hunkered, preparing to pounce. The man, who had to be around my age, lifted both hands.

"I'm...I'm sorry. I don't know what came over me." His bottom lip quivered, and the tantalizing yet sharp scent of citrus mixed with ozone reached my nose.

Fear.

I refused to become a bully, especially when this man was clearly struggling with being turned.

Ryker and the others reached us, and I looked at each of them, wanting to communicate somehow that this man wasn't a risk after all, when the bastard lunged at me once more.

I stumbled back, but my injured shoulder prevented me from moving quickly enough.

As my attacker's teeth sank into my neck, cold realization settled over me. This was it. This was my end.

But instead of ripping out my throat, he began sucking my blood.

He wanted to drain me.

Realizing he'd been overcome by bloodlust, I reached up to claw his face, but a large chestnut-brown wolf soared past my eyes, the scent immediately telling me who it was.

Ryker.

He ripped out the vampire's throat.

Blood spilled all over my chest and front legs as the halfling retracted his teeth and desperately grasped his neck, trying to stop the blood flow.

As the blood continued to gush between his fingers, he fell on his ass, and Ryker moved to stand between us. Out of the corner of my eye, I saw Kendric, Xander, and Gage circle the dying attacker.

My lungs wanted to burst, but at the same time, I couldn't fill them with air. The world underneath me quaked, making it hard to balance. No one else seemed to be having an issue, which meant I was growing weak *again*.

I didn't understand what the hell had just happened. Vampires were supposed to only be born, not created, but this person had clearly been in transition and not in his right mind. I hadn't even sensed the threat coming, which spoke volumes about the mysterious stalker I'd thought I sensed earlier. Clearly, something *was* wrong with me.

The moment the man quit wheezing and his heart stopped, the pain from my injuries roared to life. Ryker turned toward me, the sheen disappearing from his eyes and turning the brown so bright that his entire iris appeared gold. Something in me tugged toward him, but when I tried to move, my shoulder burned as though it might come unglued.

Concern darkened his eyes, and he trotted toward some larger oak trees twenty yards away.

I wanted to call after him not to go, which was incredibly stupid. Thankfully, I couldn't communicate with him in this form. I only hoped my whimpers would be mistaken for a reaction to my physical injuries and not my disappointment.

The remaining three wolf shifters' attention homed in on me for a moment, and Gage slid in to take Ryker's spot, trying to block me from the view.

Not wanting to see the dead man anyway, I closed my eyes and tried to center my thoughts. I was too injured to shift back into human form, and we had to be at least two miles from the vampire mansion. The thought of making that journey left me damn near in tears.

The rustling of human feet had me turning in the direction Ryker had gone, and what I saw made my jaw drop.

Ryker marched toward me, naked, his entire focus locked on me.

I'd felt his muscles through his clothes, but nothing prepared me for the sight before my eyes. His six-pack flexed with each step, and the curve of his muscles made my heart skip a beat.

He strode over to me, the sheen in his eyes now so thick that I couldn't make out the actual color.

"Like what you see, Rebel?" he rasped and clenched his jaw. Then he glanced at the wolves. "I double-checked and didn't find anyone else either."

Thank Fate I was in wolf form because I had no doubt that my entire body would be flushed from both desire and embarrassment. Of course the jackass would call me out on it.

I *hmph*ed, and pain slammed through my shoulder and neck from my injuries. The blood in my fur already felt gooey, courtesy of the cold weather.

I wanted to close my eyes and sleep.

Shaking my head, I tried to clear my mind, but suddenly, strong arms lifted me and cradled me like a princess despite my being in animal form.

Ryker's warm chest pressed into my body, and my eyes widened as his gaze locked with mine. I didn't like being on my back in a submissive position to him. I tried to squirm out of his hold, but that put pressure on my injured limb. A faint whine escaped before I could hide it.

"Dammit, Ember. I'm carrying you like this so I don't put pressure on your injuries." His fingers dug into my fur and skin, and a knot of desire formed in my stomach. He continued, "Stop fighting me on everything, please. You can't shift, you're severely injured, and you're still not completely healed from the attack on your pack. Let me help."

Help.

The word used to mean something positive for me, but right now, it made me feel even weaker.

I was ready to fight like hell to break free, damn the consequences, when the sheen pulled back from his eyes until it was faint. Tingles from our connection sprang up between us once again, making me immobile. My head spun from the injuries and loss of blood, and I rested it against his shoulder.

He let out a breath, and I inhaled a pleasant, minty smell that was so much better than the scent of human-vampire blood.

His eyes glowed, indicating he was speaking to the other pack members, and then we started moving. Resigning myself to the fact that I couldn't stand on my own, I decided I would allow him this.

Not because I trusted him but because I had to believe that he wouldn't betray our alliance. At least, not yet. He clearly wanted my help for the meeting with the alphas in two days' time.

After a while, my body relaxed in his arms, and I heard the patter of the other three wolves scouting around us.

Ryker's cadence lulled me into a calm that helped ease the throbbing from my injuries. I wasn't sure how long he carried me, but suddenly, a low, menacing growl emanated from Ryker, vibrating against my head.

I opened my eyes just as a sickeningly sweet smell hit my nose—activated vampire magic.

"What happened? We heard a commotion and—" Raven started but cut herself off as she and twenty other vampires in dark clothing came to a stop before us. Her hair was messy from her run, and her irises were lined with crimson, her fangs elongated.

"Don't pretend like you don't know," Ryker gritted out, his chest heaving. "And here I thought we could trust you. We're getting our vehicle and leaving immediately."

I realized that every single vampire here could now see

Ryker completely naked. My wolf snapped her teeth in my head, and anger fueled my blood.

"You *can* trust me." Raven raised both hands in surrender. "We heard howls, so we rushed out to check on you. I shouldn't have allowed you to leave so quickly—the guards haven't yet reinforced the perimeter this far out. I should've known you'd have to go farther out for hunting, but the five of you looked so rough." She shook her head and then sniffed; her gaze immediately shot to me. Eyes bulging, she gasped. "What happened?"

From what I could tell, there wasn't a hint of a lie, but my nose was still filled with Ryker and blood.

Kendric, Gage, and Xander emerged from the woods, wolf bodies tense, ready for an attack.

"A *fucking* transforming human attacked her," Ryker spat, and the thrumming that had been charging between us dimmed. "And based on the location, time, and proximity, there's only one place where that transformation could have occurred."

Her head snapped back, but just when I expected her to tell the guards to attack, she did something surprising.

She spun around, hair billowing like a curtain, and snarled, "Was anyone aware of a changeling?"

Changelings were one of the most dangerous supernaturals to exist. The human blood that still fueled them made them enormously strong and faster than should be physically possible. That had to be how he'd snuck up on me—that and my being focused on the deer.

One by one, she studied each guard. Each one shook their head...until the shortest male on the end averted his eyes.

In a flash, Raven stood in front of him and grabbed him

by his throat, lifting him so his feet dangled. He began to choke, but she didn't flinch.

"I'm going to ask you one more time, and if you don't tell me the truth, I will *end* you." Raven dug her fingernails into the guard's skin, his crimson blood trickling down his neck. "Do you know who made the changeling?"

He shook his head, though I could hear his heart rate increase and smell the sulfur of the lie.

She shrugged. "I warned you."

Before she could do anything, he croaked, "Wait."

She tilted her head. "If the first word out of your mouth isn't a name, I will kill you without an ounce of remorse."

He nodded, and as soon as she released him, he crumpled, taking a huge lungful of air. "Felix."

A few gasps came from the guards, and Raven shook her head.

I wanted to ask what that meant, but I couldn't form the words—literally—in wolf form.

"The queen's son?" Ryker scoffed bitterly, causing pain to shoot down my arm. "Why am I not surprised? He was targeting us, and he hates us as much as the guards do."

My mouth dried. Why in the world did her son hate us so much if the queen was our ally?

"Don't worry. The queen won't tolerate it, even from her own blood." Raven then used her nails to slash the shorter guard's throat.

My stomach roiled from all the violence I'd been subjected to during the past week. Before this week, I'd witnessed only two acts of violence in my entire life, each due to an alpha thinking he could take over our pack. Though Dad hadn't killed them, he had severely beaten them.

The guard's eyes widened, and he gurgled something I couldn't make out.

"That was for knowing there was a changeling created and not handling it before you left the mansion to join our search." Raven wiped the blood on her dress. "Everyone had better remember that no one is above the queen's law, not even her own children. Gerald, head back now and deal with this."

The tallest guard, who had almost translucent skin, nodded before turning and dashing back in the direction of the mansion, leaving the other eighteen waiting for orders.

"To ensure there aren't any additional turned humans on the loose, scope out the area and protect the perimeter. We don't need crazed changelings running around and making it to the city." Raven hung her head as the eighteen other vampires followed her order, spreading out in the direction the five of us had come from.

Once they vanished from sight, she turned back around and frowned. "I'm so sorry, Ember. This should never have happened. We'll make sure Felix is punished for the crime he's committed."

I hated that she could now see Ryker in all his glory. If she didn't stop staring at him, I might attack her, and there was no telling what my punishment would be.

The other three guys inched closer, Kendric coming to Raven's side. She placed a hand on his fur, causing my blood to cool and my wolf to calm.

"How do we know that won't happen again?" Ryker asked, not budging.

"Because, as soon as we get back, I'll call the queen and make sure to stream his punishment worldwide." Raven shrugged as if it weren't a big deal. "What's right is right, and he broke the law."

Somehow, that answer must have worked for Ryker because he began walking once more.

After what felt like forever, we finally reached the mansion where Lucinda, Bella, and Martin stood outside, waiting for us.

As soon as we approached, Lucinda wrinkled her nose. "The queen has decided that Felix should be beaten to near death and thrown into prison. She wants you to administer the punishment. We have the video set up, and Felix is chained in front of Her Majesty's statue."

Ryker's arms tightened. "I want Xander, Gage, and Kendric to watch the punishment, too, and ensure the vampires here at least have the appropriate reaction."

"And what will you do?" Martin arched his brow, and when his gaze settled on me, he smiled.

"Watch Ember since she's injured and needs to rest." He moved to the glass door, not waiting for permission.

Within a few seconds, he'd placed me on one of the beds. I whimpered, not wanting to dirty the sheets, but he slid in next to me and held me against him.

"Shh, Rebel. Don't fight me. Not tonight, please." He sighed. "Just get some sleep."

For some reason, I obeyed, and the thrum between us soared to life once again. Before I realized what was happening, I'd fallen asleep.

———

A loud snore roared in my ear, and my eyes popped open. For a moment, I couldn't remember where I was, and then I smelled Ryker. My head lay on his chest, bobbing with each breath he took.

Then I felt something hard against my thigh.

CHAPTER TWENTY-ONE

I blinked a few times, trying to understand how this was even possible. I'd shifted back into my human form at some point, and now I lay naked with Ryker, cuddled into his chest with his hard dick pressing into my thigh.

Not only that, but my body tingled everywhere our skin touched, making me wonder if I was on wolfsbane or something similar. None of this should've been possible. The last time I'd shifted in my sleep, I'd been a child—shifters only shifted when they felt safe, and being asleep was when we were most vulnerable.

Obviously, I didn't feel safe around *him*. The only reason I could think of that I'd done it was for healing. Shifting made the magic surge through our bodies and helped with healing if an injury wasn't too severe.

He snored faintly again, and I lifted my head to find his face completely relaxed. My heart stopped as I took in every inch of his perfect features. When he was awake, he always wore a scowl or a tense expression. But now, he looked at peace...and even more handsome.

"And here I thought I stood a chance," Gage whispered, causing my head to snap in his direction.

Both brows were raised, and his lips were pressed into a firm line.

Stomach sinking, I wanted to disappear. I couldn't believe I'd gotten caught not only cuddling with Ryker but watching him sleep. How creepy was *that,* and how much worse could this get?

I opened my mouth to respond, but Ryker's breathing quickened like he might be waking.

Dammit, Fate! She took me up on my challenge, proving that the situation could, in fact, get worse.

I tried disentangling the leg I'd thrown over his waist, but his arms tightened around me, holding me in place. There was no graceful way of getting out of this without things becoming more awkward.

He groaned, and his eyes fluttered open. A small smile tugged on the corners of his mouth until the sheen that kept randomly appearing hid the color of his eyes once more and the tingles between us eased, though they didn't fully disappear.

We jerked away from each other. I rolled toward the end of the bed, but my injuries ached, causing me to not be able to catch myself properly on my left side.

My naked ass hit the floor. There was movement on top of the mattress, no doubt from Ryker, as Gage rushed to my side.

He squatted beside me, taking my arm. I tried to cover my breasts, my pack's usual modesty kicking in.

"You are so injury-prone." Gage shook his head, trying to help me to my feet.

The movement caused discomfort, and I groaned before I could stop myself.

Ryker leaped out of bed to my side and landed on his feet. He was still completely naked, and from my precarious position on the floor, his still-hard penis was right in my face, and, boy...it was *large*.

He shoved Gage in the chest hard enough that Gage released my arm, and I fell back on my bottom. My body jerked, and my shoulder and throat throbbed. It would probably be another day before I felt completely normal.

"Don't *touch* her, and get out of the fucking room," Ryker commanded as he slid between Gage and me. Now his tight ass was in my face, and I wasn't sure which side I enjoyed staring at more.

"Whoa." Gage shuffled backward a few steps. "I was just trying to help her up. She's got to be exhausted, especially since she didn't eat last night."

Ryker clenched his fists at his sides. "*I* will take care of her. You need to leave. *Now*."

"Man, this is our room too. It's not just yours." Gage sighed, but his voice lowered in defeat. "I just came in to check on her. We've all been worried about her."

My stomach fluttered, and I scolded myself for it. Just because they said they cared now didn't mean it would always be that way. I had to remember that. Look at what Reid had done.

Taking a deep breath, Ryker relaxed marginally. "I understand, but this isn't a normal situation. Go get her something to eat, and I'll bring her out after she gets some clothes on."

Gage moved a few steps, and Ryker mirrored each one, blocking his view of me the best he could. Around him, I managed to see Gage shake his head and mutter, "If I didn't know any better, I'd think you two were fated mates." He walked out and slammed the door.

The room shook a little, and both Ryker and I remained exactly where we were as silence fell. My wolf tried to inch forward and make me close the distance between us, but I gritted my teeth, forcing myself to remain in place.

"For the love of Fate, can you *please* put some clothes on?" He kept his back to me, but his hands once again fisted at his sides. "I'm not sure I can keep myself under control if anyone else comes in here."

I wasn't sure how to respond, so I climbed to my feet and searched for something to put on.

"Your bag is under your side of the bed."

A thrill shot through me.

My side of the bed.

I froze. The last thing I needed was to feel any sort of positive emotion toward him. Gage was so out of line by saying Ryker was acting like my fated mate. Ryker clearly hated me and kept me around only because of my pack link with Briar.

Kneeling, I pulled my bag out and located a bra, panties, a maroon shirt, and jeans to wear. I quickly pulled them on, thankful that the shift back to human form had removed the blood that covered me despite the stains on the sheets. And then I ran my fingers through my hair, trying to tame it. "I'm dressed."

"Thank Fate." He spun around, giving me a side view of his ass and penis, which was still hard.

Deep need throbbed within me, catching me off guard. I sat on the edge of the bed, closing my eyes and gripping the side of the mattress, trying to calm the desire rolling through me before he could smell it.

I could hear him behind me on the other side of the bed, and I hated how the image of his naked body kept replaying in my mind. I needed to not think about that because nothing would ever happen between us.

Ever.

When I heard his zipper, I finally opened my eyes, knowing that at least half his body had to be covered.

The spicy scent of desire drifted over—from *him.*

My wolf howled in response, but I gripped the edge of the mattress even harder. Even if he was aroused, having sex would complicate matters and distract me. I had to remain focused on the goal and not do something that would potentially risk my sister. I couldn't lose her.

He moved back in my direction. Not wanting him to know I was affected by him too, I bit the inside of my cheek. I whimpered, pressing harder than intended, and suddenly his scent filled my nose.

His hands cupped my face and lifted it gently upward as he rasped, "What's wrong?"

The gold in his eyes was like flames on a candle, mesmerizing me. I could feel my pulse quicken, and I knew I needed to move away, but somehow, I couldn't budge.

"Are your injuries still bothering you?" he asked as his focus dropped to my neck. It continued lower to where my breasts pressed against the *V* of my shirt.

Right. He'd asked me a question. I should probably answer. "No, I bit the inside of my cheek." I winced, realizing how lame I sounded, but at least it was an answer.

His gaze flicked to my mouth, and I licked my lips.

The intoxicating smell of desire swirled from both of us. My lungs stopped working as the buzzing from his touch jolted through my cheeks and ran through my entire body. All I could focus on was his full lips, wondering if they would taste as minty as his breath.

He lowered his head, and my mind screamed *move,* but

my body didn't budge. I took a jerky breath as his lips touched mine, causing tingles to run through my mouth.

The door swung open, and Ryker stumbled back, ruining the moment.

I didn't move an inch, trying to understand what had just happened as Xander strolled through.

"You two are up. Finally." Xander rubbed his hands together.

Ryker's nostrils flared. "Does no one know how to knock around here?"

"Uh…when did knocking become a necessity?" Xander tilted his head, but I knew the moment he smelled the one thing we couldn't hide—the scent. It hadn't had time to dissipate. "Oh…I—"

For the hundredth time, I wanted to disappear. "Of course you don't need to knock," I blurted, trying to salvage the moment. I hated how vulnerable and foolish I'd been with Ryker, and when I glanced at him and saw the sheen back over his eyes, my wolf sighed.

"We'll get it resolved now once and for all." Ryker waved to us to follow him and marched out the door toward the kitchen.

Both Xander and I stared at each other.

Ryker cleared his throat from the other room. "You two get in here. I want everyone to hear exactly what I have to say to ensure there is *no* misunderstanding."

"That means hurry." Xander rolled his eyes.

After the awkward exchange we'd just had, I was eager to remove myself from the scene of the crime. I hurried into the kitchen with Xander right behind me to find Gage cooking on the gas stove against the wall and Kendric and Raven sitting on the barstools on the far side of the island.

The room spun a little, but I made my way to the edge

of the marble island and held it to support myself. I needed calories because I hadn't eaten in a while, and my body was recovering from extensive injuries. Even my wolf's magic didn't feel as strong despite her making her presence known just moments ago.

Raven homed in on me as if she could tell there was something wrong.

When Ryker began talking, I wanted to hug him for keeping her from asking questions about why I was clutching the counter.

Wait. No. I definitely couldn't want to hug him, right?

"Now that we have Rebel, we should establish rules of etiquette so no one accidentally walks in on her." Ryker moved to stand between the back counter and the island, across from Kendric and a few feet from Gage.

The scent of meat hit my nose. My stomach gurgled, followed by sharp hunger pains, and I noted Gage was searing two pieces of steak.

"Since there's a woman staying with us, knocking on the bedroom door before entering is now required." Ryker crossed his arms. "Gage walked in on her completely *naked*."

"Man, you were in there too." Gage flipped the steaks, cooking the other side. "In fact, you were in bed with her while you *both* were naked."

Smirking, Raven leaned back in her seat while Kendric rubbed his temples.

"Wait." Xander pointed to the bedroom door. "Is that why you told me to go in there and get them? I thought it was because we couldn't pack-link with Ember."

Kendric hung his head. "He didn't have to pack-link with her while Ryker was with her."

"Why couldn't you just holler at us?" I didn't understand what sort of game or logic they were employing.

"The rooms are soundproof when the doors are closed," Raven explained and lifted a wine glass full of red liquid emanating the coppery, sweaty scent of human blood. "Otherwise, you wouldn't have been able to sleep last night with all the commotion outside."

"Commotion? There was more than the attack on us?" My mouth went dry. What had I missed?

"She means Felix's punishment." Kendric rolled his shoulders back and wrinkled his nose. "It was pretty brutal. If he hadn't been a descendant of the royal line, he would've died."

My knees gave out, but luckily, I was still holding the edge of the island. I wasn't sure what shocked me most—the queen having her own son beaten almost to death or him still being alive. "Where is he?"

"The offsite prison." Raven set her glass on the counter. "He's far away, so you're safe here now."

"And the queen made her point." Gage snagged two plates from a cabinet and slid a medium-rare steak onto each one. "I suspect no one will dare make another changeling anytime soon." He placed one steak in front of me.

My left hand grabbed the steak and brought it to my lips. I took a huge bite and chewed, enjoying the juices as the meat slid down my throat. My stomach rumbled eagerly, and I took another bite.

I'd never been this hungry before, and the sensation was completely unnerving.

"Here." Ryker placed his plate next to mine. "Eat this one too."

Xander inhaled as Gage's eyebrows rose to an almost comical level.

Despite my mouth being full, I shook my head. I swallowed. "You need food too." He hadn't eaten in a while either.

"I've been craving beef jerky." He pressed his lips together and headed back into the bedroom, where I heard him open a bag.

I couldn't stop eating. I took another large bite, eager to get as much in me as quickly as possible.

"Whoa." Xander hurried past Gage and to the refrigerator and removed a bottle of water. "Drink this before you choke." He then rolled the bottle down the island toward me.

Silence descended as Ryker came back in eating jerky, and I devoured the two steaks and drained the entire bottle of water. When I finished, my stomach seemed to have expanded, indicating I might have eaten too much.

"Are you okay?" Ryker asked then took the last bite of his third jerky stick.

"I'm fine." I smiled, but I kept a firm grip on the counter with my right hand just in case.

"Now that you two are done, Ryker, the queen wants to speak to you and the rest of your pack." Raven drained her glass. "She wants to discuss the meeting in a couple days as well as hear what happened with the changeling."

I pushed off the counter, needing to show them and myself that I was fine. "Sounds good to me."

"She wants to speak to them—not you." Raven cringed a little. "She said that she wants you to rest, especially after an attack like that. It was brutal."

My blood ran cold. I didn't like being excluded from that meeting.

"She's right." Ryker nodded, glancing at me. "Besides, we're the ones who have a relationship with her. She trusts our judgment but probably not yours yet."

That made sense, but something didn't quite feel right about it all.

"But I don't want Ember on her own without one of us with her, so—" Ryker started.

"I'll stay." Raven typed into her phone and hit send. "I'll make sure nothing happens to her. The queen will be waiting for you in the study. She told me to inform her when you guys are ready." Her phone dinged, and she held it up, revealing the message: **I'm logging into the call now.**

"Okay. We shouldn't be long." Ryker bit his bottom lip before heading out of the kitchen without a second glance in my direction.

Kendric kissed Raven's cheek, and the three Grimstone members followed their alpha.

Great. Things between Ryker and me were going to be even more strange, and he'd excluded me and left me alone with a vampire. If he wasn't getting back at me for groping him while I was asleep, I didn't know what he was thinking.

I couldn't hide a yawn. "I guess I'll go back into the bedroom." I didn't want to stand here and have a stilted conversation.

"Wait." Raven blurred to my side.

She glanced in the direction the men had gone. When her attention settled back on me, a tinge of red outlined her irises.

Holy shit. She was channeling her vampire magic. What the hell did the vampires have in store for me now?

CHAPTER TWENTY-TWO

My wolf inched forward, ready to push Raven's magic off me. If she attacked, I wouldn't have time to shift. I almost called out for Ryker and the others, but I kept my mouth shut, not wanting to put them in the middle of whatever this was.

Obviously, the vampires had it out for me, and I needed someone to continue the search for Briar. I hoped those four would.

I clutched the plate in case I needed it to defend myself.

Raven's eyes returned to their normal shade, and she propped her weight to one side and placed a hand on her hip. "You think a plate would keep me from killing you?" She wrinkled her nose, scanning me.

I huffed, trying to hide the fact that a chill ran down my spine. She was far too observant. "What are you going to do?" I whispered as the men vanished from sight.

She rolled her eyes. "Are you always this dramatic, or is it because you're weak and vulnerable?"

My wolf growled, the sound vibrating in my chest. I hated feeling weak and getting called out on it made me want to prove that I wasn't, which was stupid. I *knew* I wasn't up to snuff. "Just do whatever you're going to do and get it over with."

Tsking, she looped her arm through mine to support my weight. She then led me into the bedroom where the five of us were staying. She pushed me toward my bed and shut the door.

That made sense. There was no risk of the guys overhearing us and intervening in here.

My heartbeat quickened, so I tried taking a deep breath to calm down. A predator always loved it when the prey became scared, and I refused to allow her to enjoy this moment more than she already would.

"No harm will come to you, Ember." Raven chuckled, shaking her head. "I just want to speak to you alone."

I tilted my head and blinked. "What do you mean?" Her wording had been precise, and thanks to the lack of sulfur in the air, I trusted her.

Taking a few steps toward me, she lifted both hands like she was coming toward a scared animal. "There's something off with Ryker. There has been for a few months now. It began a few days after he first arrived here when he left on his own to run an errand."

"Why are you telling me this instead of discussing it with him?" There were so many red flags being tossed around right now, but I couldn't deny that I was curious.

"Because he's keeping it from his pack, and there's no way he'll be willing to tell anyone outside them." She lowered her head and sighed. "In fact, it's caused problems between Kendric and me because he's adamant that there isn't anything wrong. He claims it's how Ryker is choosing to process his grief, and when I tried to push it..."

Silence filled the space between us.

"Why do you think something's off?" If his pack members didn't feel there was anything wrong, then there most likely wasn't. "They would know best."

"You must swear to keep what I'm about to tell you a secret." She swallowed hard. "If you won't, then I won't be able to share this information with you."

My head tilted back, and my breath caught. I never would've believed that a vampire and wolf shifter would confide in each other. Granted, I wouldn't have believed that the royal pack and my own would get slaughtered either, so exceptions were pretty much the rule lately.

Because of this, I found myself nodding. "I swear." Whatever information she had, I needed to know. Ryker had been acting irrationally, and I was banking on his pack to help me locate and save Briar.

She licked her lips, one of her canines pressing into the side. "You know how the queen mentioned there are magical wards around the area to warn us of a threat?"

"Yeah." My knees finally succumbed to weakness and gave out, but luckily, my bottom hit the mattress.

"Well, they also tell us when someone has trace magic on them, even when they're not a threat to our kind. Ryker didn't trigger them when he first arrived, but that day, when he returned, one of the magical wards notified the queen."

I placed my hands on the mattress to hold myself up. "And she didn't confront him?"

"She'd already left the mansion to head to Garnerville, but she called me and Lucinda. That's one reason that the guards don't trust him. Since it isn't threatening magic, we're trying to not break the peace with the pack. However, Ryker hasn't been quite the same as he used to be when he would come here with the royals for meetings."

My gut knotted. "You have no clue what it's like to

experience what we have. The bonds between pack members are pre...cious," I said brokenly, trying to hold back my emotions. "Losing even one is devastating, let alone almost all of them—" My vision blurred, and a tear trickled down my cheek. If I tried to continue, I would fall apart, and I'd already shown too much weakness in front of everyone.

"I've experienced more loss than you realize." Raven's expression became strained. "But it's more than that, Ember. He's got some sort of spell on him. And there's a darkness to him that wasn't there before. When he came here after the *incident,* he was grieving, and then he came back from his 'errand' as a man with revenge as his primary focus. It was like something inside him snapped."

"I'm pushing my grief away too." I wiped away more tears as they continued to come. "So I can't condemn him for doing what he needed to do to get by."

She shook her head. "You still feel it. It almost seems like he *can't* sense it, which is a huge problem."

My heart twisted. I couldn't imagine forcing myself not to feel anything for the cold voids in my chest. It would be an insult to my pack, and I planned to grieve for each and every one of them once I got Briar back. "Right now, I don't have time to deal with Ryker and his problems. I have to find my sister and get her someplace safe so we can grieve and move on with our own lives."

Placing a hand on my shoulder, she pressed her lips together. "That's a noble goal but, Ember, whoever is doing this needs to be stopped. Who says they won't continue to look for you? Your existence and the fact that royal blood, faint though it may be, runs through you—you have the right to challenge anyone who claims the top spot. Even your sister and your descendants will be a threat, so hiding won't solve anything."

Fuck. She was right. I hadn't thought about it like that, but an alpha willing to go for the throne would want to eliminate any competition. That was the whole reason for this meeting in two days. "Finding my sister is my first priority."

"I understand that, but this meeting will help with both of your objectives." She dropped her hand, making me realize that the coolness of her touch had seeped through my shirt to my skin. "I just need you to help us figure out what's going on with Ryker. Whatever it is has made him colder and more detached each time we see him. It could harm your mission if he continues down this path."

I hated that she was right, but I could see her point. Witnessing what he'd done to Simon, who'd just been in the wrong place at the wrong time, turned my stomach. That could've been anyone—including me and my sister. Hell, he'd pulled me out of the river, but I might have died if the other three hadn't been there to pressure him to take me to their cabin.

If Ryker decided he wanted to ascend the throne, and he had some sort of witch influence over him, there was no telling what rules he might implement on the packs. "I can try, but no promises."

"Fill us in on anything you learn, please." She smiled sadly. "I'm sorry to ask this of you, but we need the alliance between vampires and shifters to remain. It's best for both species, and Queen Ambrosia cares for every supernatural and their well-being."

For some reason, I was actually beginning to believe it.

"Get some rest. You need it. Every vampire here can smell how weak your blood is." She went to the door and paused. "I'll make sure one of the quadruplets cooks for you and brings the food to you here in a little bit."

A part of me wanted to refuse, tell her that I'd shift and hunt, but I didn't want to go back into the woods. I didn't want to risk something else happening before the meeting. I had to be there. If I could get any hint as to who had Briar and where they were keeping her, I needed to be fully healed and alert. "Thank you. That sounds great."

She winked and left the room, shutting the door behind her.

Not bothering to switch beds—Ryker could do it if he wanted to—I plopped down where I'd slept the night before. With a full stomach and the lingering scent of Ryker on the sheets, I fell quickly to sleep.

Two nights later, I was rubbing my sweaty palms on my jeans as Ryker and I pulled into the parking lot of the bar.

The past two days had been full of rest, eating, and trying to ignore the growing strange feelings I had around Ryker. Much to my surprise, he'd continued to sleep in the same bed as me, though we'd remained fully clothed. Still, each morning, I'd had to pry my body away from him because we had closed the distance between us.

Gage, Kendric, and Xander had hung out with the vampires, but Ryker had left each day to search the woods for more threats, leaving me alone. That gave me time to focus on my connection with Briar, and I had a pretty good inkling that she was somewhere to the west of us. That also informed me which three packs could be working with Reid to hide her.

The one unexpected yet pleasant spot was that Raven

visited with me for a couple of hours each day, and I'd learned that we had a lot in common. She'd even dragged me into the kitchen to make caramel brownie cheesecake from scratch, which both the vampires and the guys had devoured. The simple task had made things feel sort of normal though the flashbacks of my pack and family kept coming.

"It's going to be okay." Ryker pulled into a spot and turned off the SUV. "Xander, Gage, and Kendric are on their way to check out the three packs, so if we can determine which is most likely to have Briar, they can scout around until we can get there."

"I know. That doesn't mean that I don't dread this." I glanced at the time, noting we were exactly ten minutes late. Our plan was to let the gathered alphas get comfortable and start discussions, believing that Ryker wasn't coming.

I scanned the upscale, log-cabin-style bar. It had been tied to the royals for generations and had an elegant, rustic feel that screamed *wolf*. "I doubt the Van Eatons are the ones who have her." They were a similar pack to us that didn't like to get involved with stupid politics and tended to keep to themselves.

Ryker got out of the vehicle and walked around the front in my direction, closest to the gigantic wooden doors.

I filled my lungs, dreading facing Reid and his family after what they'd done. I had to hold myself together, but all I wanted to do was rip out his throat. And worse, I knew when I saw him, the stupid fated-mate connection would flare up inside me, making me want him despite all that shit.

It was beyond messed up, and I channeled that hatred toward Fate.

Ryker appeared at my door and opened it, startling me and setting my blood boiling. How was I going to be able to

determine who had Briar if I couldn't even focus on immi-
nent threats and keep my head grounded?

"Are you coming?" Ryker's brows furrowed. "You're
just sitting here."

The sheen over his eyes hid their natural color. What
the hell was going on? Could it have something to do with
whatever spell had been cast on him? But no one else had
noticed it, so maybe I was being paranoid again.

"Sorry." I shook my head, letting my red hair shake out
and fall over my shoulders, contrasting with the emerald
shade of the dress that Raven had forced me to wear for this.
I climbed from the vehicle, balancing on my black wedges.
"I just dread seeing all of them."

He shut the door, and I forced myself to say, "Thanks."

"No big deal. Just playing the part of a doting
boyfriend." He shrugged, taking my hand and leading me to
the door.

I tried to ignore the way my hand tingled in his and
keep pace with him. Even worse, I hated that I felt safe
with him.

When we reached the door, a note stated **Closed
until 6 PM for a professional meeting.** In other
words, there would be only shifters in attendance, with no
humans to interfere.

Loud voices boomed from inside.

Ryker turned toward me. "Are you ready for this?"

No. I wasn't. This was the very last thing I wanted to do
—face Reid, who'd rejected me and taken part in slaughtering my pack. But I would do it for Briar. "As ready as I'll
ever be."

He sniffed, searching for the smell of a lie, and nodded.
"Let's do this." Then he opened the door.

Five tables had been pushed together in the center of

the massive bar, three huge windows that overlooked the mountains across from them. However, the gorgeous view wasn't what held everyone's attention. In fact, the entire place went quiet as all twenty alphas stared at the two of us on the threshold.

Traitorously, my eyes located Reid...and then I couldn't believe what happened.

CHAPTER TWENTY-THREE

Nothing.

I waited for the inevitable pain, but *nothing* flared inside me until his undeniable scent hit my nose... mixed with someone else's.

I inhaled shakily. He'd completed a mate bond with someone else.

Four of the five men who sat with their backs to the window had creased brows, which made sense since we didn't know each other except for the Shae pack alpha, Bruce, on the other end. His expression looked slightly pained.

Reid's eyes widened. Ryker tugged me closer to his side and wrapped an arm around my waist, his warmth searing into me.

My attention couldn't be diverted from Reid. My blood boiled. The sensations of pain and heartbreak didn't hit me like I'd expected. Instead, my legs felt like Jell-O, allowing Ryker to maneuver me with our sides pressed together, no space between us.

Even without the buzz that sometimes sprang up

between us, my pulse quickened. I was enjoying his touch way too much. I hated that he had this effect on me despite all the awful things he'd done. For some reason, a growing piece of me wanted to believe he had good reason for his actions, but...torturing innocents was wrong, no matter what.

From his seat at the center of the table, Reid jumped to his feet, his chair skidding back. "Ember! You're alive," he rasped.

I laughed, letting all my hatred and bitterness show. "Disappointed?"

He blinked and shook his head. "What do—"

"Let's cut to the chase because Ember and I have other things to do." Ryker glanced at me and winked, causing my heart to skip a beat.

I had to get my head on straight. This was pretend, but the faint, spicy scent of his arousal hit my nose. When his mouth touched mine, a jolt went straight through my stomach. Then his tongue brushed my lips, demanding entrance.

I inhaled shakily, and as soon as it registered that I should respond, he pulled away and arched a brow at the place full of male alphas. "I assume this meeting is to discuss who the next royals will be?"

Perry leaned over the table from his position next to his son. He scowled. "Yes, that's the topic of discussion. We assumed you weren't coming, so we began. These attacks are horrendous and must be stopped."

There was no scent of a lie, and a chill ran down my spine despite the fury blazing inside me. I gritted my teeth and jerked forward, wanting to punch the bastard in the jaw. However, Ryker's arm tightened around my waist like a vise, keeping me anchored at his side. The way Perry and

Reid wrinkled their noses in disgust made me want to kill them both right then and there.

How dare they look at me like *I* was the problem?

"Sorry, Rebel's a little feisty. One of the things I admire most about her." Ryker chuckled. He moved his lips next to my ear and breathed, "Calm down. Remember what your number one goal is—Briar."

My sister's name echoed in my head. He was right. The point was to stay focused and unaffected to infuriate the others—like we had no worries about being in control. We'd been here a minute, and I was already ruining that.

I took a shaky breath and forced a smile. "Sorry. It's just hard seeing everyone after the loss of my pack."

"It was a travesty." Reid's face crumpled. "All those bodies... Our pack buried them this morning. Though someone had begun digging a grave, which surprised us. At least now we know who." He gestured to me.

This prick slaughtered my pack, kidnapped my sister, and now wanted to pretend to be some sort of saint by burying the people he'd murdered? Hatred punched into my stomach, making my chest tighten. I'd never realized I was so capable of these horrible sinking emotions.

From the other side of Perry, the middle-aged, light-blond-haired alpha of the Golden pack— another of the packs we were here to observe—cleared his throat. "That's awfully kind, but clearly there were survivors. How many bodies were missing?" He glanced at the Blackwoods for the answer instead of me.

I growled, unable to hide my disdain. I would know better than those two, seeing as I was part of the pack. Despite it being the twenty-first century, sexism still thrived in the shifter community.

"Me and my sister Briar. Everyone else died." My attention flickered toward Reid and Perry, hoping they could sense the disgust for them sludging through me. I watched for any reaction to my words.

Reid hung his head and flinched. "She's right. We thought they might have died elsewhere since we ran the entire perimeter of their land."

Ran was one way of putting it. The term *hunted* would have worked the best.

Every alpha nodded at Reid's confirmation, including the Asher alpha, who'd been as close to my pack as we had been to the Blackwoods. Normally, I'd brush it aside, knowing that I would either be the future beta of our pack or the alpha mate of another, but as an alpha myself, my wolf snarled.

"Of course she's right," Ryker spat. "She's the Sinclair pack alpha now. We don't need someone else confirming the numbers she stated. And don't forget she is of *royal* blood." He lifted his chin and stared down the twenty men in front of us.

My stomach fluttered. *Down, girl.* This was an act. I had to remember that. Ryker might find me attractive, but we did *not* like each other.

"There's no reason to get upset." The Hadley pack alpha lifted both hands.

"Right." Golden ran a hand through his hair, making it messy. "I just didn't know if the body count added up to the number Ember gave."

They were trying to play it off without lying, but I understood what the intention was. It had been a slight jab to undermine me because each one of these assholes wanted the crown, and none deserved it.

Bruce fidgeted, and I couldn't help but notice the sweat

beading on his brow. His milk-chocolate-brown eyes flicked toward me, and he quickly wiped his forehead.

My hands clenched. He was acting nervous, and his was one of the three packs I suspected had Briar. If it was him, then he had to be in cahoots with the Blackwoods. My stomach pitched. He was the one alpha of the three I hadn't truly suspected. He was older and had always seemed aligned with my pack's views.

The sting of betrayal hit my heart. Once again, someone I thought I knew had screwed us over.

"And she may be of *royal* blood, but we've heard the rumor that something is wrong with her," a young brown-haired man with a bowl cut spat. "No one will follow her."

Air whooshed from my lungs. Before I could say anything, Ryker released me and marched over to the prick. He got in his face and pushed his finger into Bowl Cut's chest. "There is *nothing* wrong with her. Reid was too much of an idiot to see what he could've had. She's strong, smart, and resilient. Otherwise, she wouldn't be standing here with us now."

I couldn't see Ryker's face, but I could feel alpha power pulsing from him, and my own wolf whimpered in approval. This version of Ryker didn't seem fake, but I had to push that thought away. I refused to let anyone else into my heart.

My gaze flickered to Reid, whose jaw worked as he watched the exchange. "Ember already said she doesn't want to ascend the throne, so none of this matters. We need to figure out a solution before our packs lose more strength. We can't fight an enemy as we grow weaker. Cassi mentioned a spell that can be performed so our wolf magic can identify our new leader as the new royal bloodline once we've selected them."

"If the enemy grows weaker as well, then we don't need to be in much of a hurry to make that decision." I rocked back on my heels, enjoying that the positive emotions I'd felt for Reid were now gone. I didn't give a fuck if it was because he'd mated with someone else. As long as I was free of that cursed bond, I didn't give a damn how it had happened. "*Whoever* is behind the attacks somehow diluted their scents, so they must have a witch helping them." I let the last part hang out there, especially since Reid had *just* referenced the witch tied to his pack.

Reid's and Perry's heads snapped in my direction, my implication clear. The other alphas flinched and blinked, processing what I'd just said. The Blackwoods were the rare pack that had a witch who was close to them.

"Is that your way of trying to get me back?" Reid's jaw dropped. "I know I shouldn't have embarrassed you like that, but damn, Ember. I didn't do it on purpose. You don't have to be so damn bitter."

After the slaughter of my pack, this guy had the nerve to suggest my suspicions were due to his rejection. For the first time in my life, I wanted to slit someone's throat with my bare claws. My pack strived to be pacifist and fight back only when attacked, but I believed that, for a situation like this, a change in policy would be justified.

Ryker straightened and pivoted to me. The sheen on his eyes seemed thicker than ever.

I had no clue what I'd done to get his attention, but at least this time, he'd get a show instead of being the main act. My wolf inched forward, and I marched toward Reid, but Ryker intercepted me.

I ran into his chest, and his arms circled my waist. I tried to jerk out of his grasp as he whispered, "Rebel, pretend your hatred is due to the rejection and not because you remember anything from the attack."

Shit, he was right. Now wasn't the time to act. I had my sister to save. I would take her somewhere safe and then eliminate the threat. I didn't need Reid convincing the Shae pack to harm her to get back at me.

Fighting to pull my wolf back, I forced my body to stop fighting his, but then his mouth covered mine. I gasped, but instead of air, his tongue filled my mouth, tasting of mint and honey, a combination I never imagined I'd enjoy this much.

Before I could stop myself, I responded, and my arms slid up his chest and around his neck. I anchored my body to his, and the world seemed to disappear.

Until he pulled away.

He snickered and turned his head toward Reid. "Your loss is my gain, and it's not that you rejected her that's the problem. It's that you attempted to embarrass her, which wasn't a regal move."

I smiled, immensely enjoying yet another dig we'd managed to make at Reid, one that made it clear he didn't have the temperament needed to be king.

Reid's flush and flared nostrils had me grinning so hard it hurt.

"That's quite enough!" Perry exclaimed. "You don't get to come in here and make these statements like they're facts."

"Actually, he does." An alpha with salt-and-pepper hair stood. "That's the whole purpose of the meeting, right? To discuss who makes sense to lead? The Grimstones have been running rampant, trying to pin the attacks on someone else, and the Sinclair pack was supposedly extinct. Yet here they both stand, and *you* have attempted to control this entire meeting. I drove ten hours to say that I think a competition should be held to determine the next ruler. Just because you scheduled this meeting and selected a location near your territory doesn't mean you should assume the role. You have no claim."

"What sort of competition are you suggesting?" The Golden pack alpha tilted his head. "Because I agree that the Blackwoods shouldn't use manipulation to take control, but neither should those two. Neither one of them could protect their own packs."

Both Ryker and I tensed. I wanted to scream that the attackers were the ones trying to take control, but I didn't need to.

One by one, the other alphas agreed, causing Perry's and Reid's expressions to strain further.

Good. Those assholes didn't deserve an easy win...not after everything they'd done.

"Now listen here—" Perry slammed a hand on the table.

But the Golden alpha jumped to his feet. "I can't remain here. An unknown scent has been discovered on my perimeter. I must get back to my pack."

Bruce ran a shaky hand through his dark brown hair. "Then I must get back to my pack as well since we share a border."

"If our enemy knows that the local pack alphas are meeting here, then we should have a video conference to discuss the competition." A man with sandy-blond hair stood. "We should've never left our homes with a threat at large, but the Blackwoods promised the meeting would remain secret. We should all get back to our packs imme-diately."

My stomach dropped. Was another attack happening? Thinking of another pack being slaughtered had my stomach in knots, especially knowing Kendric, Gage, and Xander were in that area too.

The Shae and Golden alphas were the first ones out the door. Ryker and I glanced at each other before trailing behind them.

We needed to follow Bruce to see where he went.

The two of us jogged to our vehicle as the other alphas rushed out. We jumped in and waited for Bruce to peel out of his spot and gun it down the road.

Ryker didn't wait long before we pulled out and followed him.

"Are the others safe?" I asked and gripped the door handle as we took a curve fast.

"They're fine. The Golden pack picked up Kendric's scent. He got too close to their lookout, trying to scout for your sister." His jaw clenched, and he kept his eyes on the road as he reached out and took my hand.

The buzz shot between us, and I couldn't make myself pull away.

"Don't worry. He's already back in his car and heading toward the Shae pack territory to meet up with Gage. They won't find him."

Some of the pressure on my shoulders lifted. I hadn't realized how worried I'd been about him.

Not wanting to distract Ryker, I kept my mouth shut, and we fell into silence.

About thirty minutes later, something hot blazed in my chest as if I were on fire.

CHAPTER TWENTY-FOUR

The warmth increased to a blaze within the coldness that had taken over where all the pack links had been. My breath caught, and I gripped my chest.

Ryker's head snapped in my direction. "What's wrong?"

"Nothing." I inhaled raggedly. "It's the opposite. I sense Briar." Tears burned my eyes, but then blurred lights hit them, followed by a honk. My pulse quickened. "Ryker!"

The vehicle jerked to the right, tires squealing. My head hit the window, causing my right ear to ring. Then the vehicle leveled out.

"Dammit, I'm sorry." Ryker pulled to the side of the road and parked. "Are you hurt?" The color of his irises seemed to twinkle in the moonlight, and my mind muddied.

I touched the side of my head, not concerned in the least. "I'm fine." I patted my chest again and smiled. "I feel Briar, but we need to get back on the road and not lose sight of the Shae alpha." I tried to link with my sister, but the connection was still muted, like she was asleep.

"Is she okay?" He touched my hand, causing a jolt to crash between us.

"I...I don't know." I could try to wake her, but I didn't want to since I wasn't sure what sort of situation she was in. If she was being tortured and had been injured, waking her up would only make things worse. "But we're getting close." Pressure released in my chest, and tears ran down my cheeks.

He nodded and squeezed my hand. "That's good. It means you were right about where you felt her connection coming from."

I bit my lip. I'd needed to hear those words even if he hadn't been sure about my sense. I hated that I wanted to lean into him and breathe in his scent, looking for comfort.

I didn't deserve comfort, not with Briar in whatever sort of predicament she was in. And I had to remember what Ryker was capable of. I'd heard the stories and had seen him torture Simon firsthand. I pulled my hand away and placed it back into my lap.

A frown tugged at his lips, but he placed his hands back on the steering wheel and pulled back onto the road. He took the next curve expertly, going a little too fast, but we needed to catch up to Bruce. "The guys are pretty confident about where they're keeping her if she's on their pack land. We'll get her free tonight."

My back straightened. "When did you hear from them?" I tried to keep my voice level and wrung my hands to calm my frustration at not being kept informed, the anxious energy of needing to see my sister flaring.

"Right before you gasped like something was wrong. None of the packs were guarding their lands as expected, and the three of them shifted and covered themselves in mud so they wouldn't be easily scented. There's some sort of small building on the back of the Shae pack territory with two people keeping watch on it."

"Small building?" I gnawed on my cheek. "Like a cell or something?" A shiver ran down my spine.

"They aren't sure." He reached over like he might go for my hand, but he hesitated. "They just noticed it and are keeping watch until we arrive."

My hand moved toward his, but I stopped myself. "You don't have to pretend to like or be concerned about me anymore. We've left the alphas."

He grimaced, replacing his hand on the steering wheel. "It wasn't pretending, Rebel."

"Oh, then what was it?" I turned toward him, hoping he'd insult me. I needed a reminder of why I shouldn't be attracted to him. "Right. It was acting...a game to make the other shifters uncomfortable while enjoying being the one with something to hold over them for once."

"It'd be easier for both of us if it were any of those things." His jaw clenched, and he gritted out, "But we both know that what happened back there has been brewing for a while. Hell, every morning, we wake up tangled around each other."

My head spun. Of everything I'd expected him to say, *that* was definitely not on the list. "You're hot—so what?" I crossed my arms, needing to restrain them in case they tried to do something stupid.

"If it were just about looks, there wouldn't be a problem between us right now." His nostrils flared, and he tightened his grip on the wheel.

Luckily, Bruce's black truck came into view again, giving me a reason to change focus and not dwell on what Ryker had just said.

No matter what I felt for him, the two of us could *never* be together. He tortured people and refused to listen to anyone else. I shouldn't be wasting any time justifying why Ryker and I couldn't be together.

Briar was my priority and deserved *all* my attention.

My fingers dug into my chest again. I was still reacclimating to the warmth of Briar's link after the sensation of icicles for so long. "What sort of shape do you think she'll be in?" My heart sank.

The rigidness of his face smoothed, and he blew out a breath. "I have no clue, but I can promise that, as long as her heart is beating, we'll get her out of there."

My bottom lip trembled, so I bit down on it. I didn't have time for fear or weakness, especially with my thoughts around *him*. "I can't lose her. Not again." A tear rolled down my cheek, and my chest felt like it would rend in two. I shivered once again.

The Shae alpha's truck slowed and turned right onto the road that led to the pack neighborhood.

"Good. He didn't notice us." Ryker let out a breath and turned left, away from their territory line, into the dirt cutoff. He drove down the bumpy road a little way, jostling me everywhere.

"Where the hell are we going?" I rasped, placing my hands on the front console, trying to remain in place.

"I'm going to park where the other three did. They gave me the coordinates." He continued on the road. It became a little choppier, but after a few seconds, it leveled out, and we reached the three other vehicles the guys had borrowed from the vampires.

Ryker stopped the SUV and cut the engine, and the world once again fell silent. The cold vibration down my spine hadn't vanished, and something seemed more off than ever.

He opened his door, but I couldn't get myself to move.

Something hung in the air around me like a warning, and the chill that ran through me seemed to freeze even more. Something about this situation didn't feel right, but I had no clue why.

Nothing seemed amiss.

Was paranoia getting the best of me again?

"Are you coming?" Ryker arched a brow, and his irises glistened. My wolf wanted to respond to him.

"Yeah." I shook my head, trying to clear it. "Sorry. I'm getting a weird feeling again."

"The guys checked out the area. All three of them got together again before they shifted to scout things out." His eyes glowed, linking with them. After a few seconds, he continued, "And they're fine now. They're still waiting for us in the same spot, and nothing has changed on their end. If I thought there was a threat, I'd tell you."

For some reason, I trusted him, and I hated myself for it. "Okay." I blew out a breath, trying to ignore the way my wolf shrank back a little. Something similar to humidity clung to my skin. I exhaled and got out of the vehicle, letting my feet hit the ground as softly as I could in case someone might hear me.

I glanced around the woods, noting that there wasn't even a hint of an animal for miles. "It's quiet out here."

"Well, if they have a witch helping them, there's no telling what sort of magic they have." He walked around to his trunk and nodded in the direction of the Shae pack's territory line. This part of the woods was public land, which was probably how they knew about this spot, assuming they'd been observing the packs while trying to figure out who'd killed the royals and their pack.

I fell into step with him, and the two of us walked quickly toward the main road that divided the public forest lands from pack territory. My eyes scanned the trees for signs of a threat.

With each step I took, the pressure on my skin seemed to intensify. I glanced over my shoulder, searching for whatever it was, and Ryker stilled.

"Fuck," he hissed and took my hand, dragging me in the very direction my senses were screaming not to go.

"Stop," I snarled, trying to fight him. I looked across the road. "What's going on—" Adrenaline pumped through me. This was about to get worse than I ever could have imagined.

The Shae alpha and at least fifty of his pack members stood across the street, blocking us from entering their territory.

"Fuck, he must have noticed us." Ryker's grip tightened on mine. "I stayed over a hundred yards behind him the entire time, and he doesn't know this vehicle."

"Maybe he saw us when we almost wrecked," I muttered, barely able to make out Ryker's words.

"Don't flatter yourself." Bruce rolled his eyes. "I already knew you suspected me before I left the meeting. Had I known that Ember had lived, I wouldn't have kept Briar here at all. I don't need any pack drama."

A sour taste filled my mouth. "Says the person who's keeping my sister hostage."

"Would you have rather I'd let her die?" Bruce wrinkled his nose. "I didn't want the death of a fellow wolf shifter on my conscience, but at the same time, I couldn't let a strange wolf run loose so she could try to claim the throne and ruin us all."

"It doesn't seem like you have a problem with threatening us, with all your shifters here facing two of us down." Ryker tensed, and the sheen covered his irises once more.

Bruce gestured to us and rasped, "You're sneaking onto my land, and Ryker has been tied to every location where a massacre has happened. Do you think I'm going to stand here and willingly put my pack at risk?"

"We just got here, and there are only two of us," Ryker replied, edging in front of me.

"You don't think we noticed the strange wolf who's been here since before the meeting or the two who joined him since then?" The Shae alpha arched a brow.

My legs almost gave out. They knew about Xander, Gage, and Kendric.

When Ryker stilled to the point of becoming a statue, I had no doubt what was going on.

"Let my pack members go," Ryker snarled.

"You come on *my* lands and command *me* to let go of three men who've been spying on my pack?" Bruce cracked his knuckles. "Not a chance in hell. I won't allow you to do to my pack what you've done to all the others. Did you really think we wouldn't keep a constant watch over our territory, knowing that if anyone found out Briar was alive, it would cause chaos?"

"We've already told people that we didn't kill our pack, Ember's, or anyone else's." Ryker's hands clenched at his side. "You're allied with the pack that's behind it all."

The Shae alpha tipped his head back. "And who would that be?"

"The Blackwood pack." I pivoted in front of Ryker as I spoke, tired of him trying to protect me. My sister was here, and Ryker's pack was in danger. I'd be damned if I remained hidden when there were people who didn't deserve to be harmed at risk. "I saw them during the attack on my pack, and there was no one else with them."

Silence descended among us. Then a shifter who had to be in his thirties whispered, "There's no smell of a lie."

"I'm aware of that." Bruce scowled and tilted his head as he examined me. "Then why didn't you tell me about it at the meeting tonight?"

"Because I didn't want to risk my sister being harmed, and we wanted to make the Blackwoods and whoever was working with them uncomfortable." This song and dance needed to end. I wanted my sister safe and sound with me. "And we determined that it was you."

He shook his head. "I'm not working with the Blackwoods—"

His words were cut off by a bloodcurdling howl.

CHAPTER TWENTY-FIVE

My stomach churned. The sound reminded me of the way my pack had howled the night they were killed. Agony rang through the howl before it abruptly cut off.

No.

This couldn't be happening.

Bruce's eyes glowed as he clutched his stomach. "We're under attack, and two of my pack members were just killed!"

My breathing increased, and my heart dropped into my stomach. I'd just gotten close to Briar—I'd be damned if I lost her again. "It's only going to get worse. You need to get your people out of here." I ran across the road, not worrying about fighting them. I needed to get to Briar.

However, four male shifters hurried in front of me and blocked my path.

I bared my teeth. "Get the fuck out of my way. I need to reach my sister."

The salt-and-pepper-haired one snarled. "This could be

a setup with your people. You're not entering our lands anywhere."

"You think I'd risk my sister to kill you all?" I huffed and clenched my hands. "How would all of you dying benefit me?"

He opened his mouth to respond when Bruce snapped, "More have died. Everyone head back to protect our pack and get them out of here."

"That's what they want." I shoved through the four men. "To lure all of you back in. You need to run and tell your pack members to get out as well." I looked forward, tugging on Briar's pack link, needing to reach her. I had visited here only once, as a child, when Dad had brought over several pack members to help the Shaes fix a flooding issue, but I'd stayed in the woods with the men and hadn't seen much of the territory.

An arm circled my waist, pulling me back.

Anger flared inside me, and I spun around, ready to punch Salt and Pepper in the jaw. When Ryker's face appeared, I stopped short.

He tugged me toward him, but I pressed my hands against his chest. "What are you *doing*?" I croaked, completely befuddled by his actions. His men were out there too, so he should be focused on getting to them just as much as I was on Briar.

"Getting you to the car so you can get the fuck out of here."

He bent to hoist me over his shoulder, and I kicked him in the chest, causing him to fall on his ass. Guilt weighed on me, but I pushed it away, focusing on what mattered in the moment. "Are you seriously trying to run to safety right now?"

Bruce and half his pack members raced past us in the

direction of the neighborhood while the rest split into two groups, running in opposite directions and circling the land. I wanted to yell at them for not listening to me, but how could I when I was doing the same thing? We were running to help the ones we loved and not leave them behind... Well, except Ryker.

Ryker jumped to his feet, eyes glowing. "I'm trying to get your ass to safety! Gage, Kendric, and Xander are getting Briar out of the holding cell right now."

"I'm not going anywhere until Briar is at my side." I spun on my heels and picked up speed in the direction the others had run. Ryker had told me enough that I had an idea of where I should be able to find Briar: at the back of the neighborhood.

I ran freely, not trying to hold my speed back like I normally did around other shifters outside my pack. This was a time I didn't care if anyone noticed I was faster than the rest of them.

"Dammit, Rebel," Ryker hissed, and then his hurried footsteps sounded behind me.

Pumping my legs, I caught up with the back of the group that was hurrying into the neighborhood. A few peeled off, and the crack of breaking bones informed me they were shifting.

I'd give anything to be able to do that, but with all these foreign wolves around me, staying in human form in case I needed to communicate was the best option for me.

My wolf whimpered as the link connecting Briar and me warmed further.

She was waking.

Cries of pain and whines of terror came more frequently, pushing me to go even faster. I gritted my teeth, and energy burst through me, increasing my speed once again. The oaks blurred as I ran, trying to reach my sister before something else happened to her.

Ember? Briar's voice rang in my head, followed by fear and hope pulsing through the pack link. *Is this a dream?*

This was far from a dream. The whole situation was another nightmare, making me relive the murder of our own pack, but I didn't want to stress her out more than she already was. *I'm here. On my way to get you.*

Two-story houses appeared, indicating that I'd reached the front of the pack neighborhood. Chaos had erupted. People with bags were running out of homes to their vehicles and throwing items in. Little kids had tears running down their faces, and another howl of agony came from somewhere on the other side of the woods.

The side close to Briar.

Ember, what's going on? Briar's anxiety spiked, causing our connection to constrict. *The screams...they sound like...*

She didn't have to say anything; I already knew and thought the same thing myself. *I'm close.* I refused to downplay the threat, but I also didn't want to confirm that our lives were at risk once again. *Are you well enough to run?* I didn't want to think about them torturing her, but at this point, I needed to know what we were up against.

Yes, I'm perfectly healthy, but— Her words cut off, and cold fear pulsed from her side.

Briar! I linked, pushing myself harder. *What's going on?*

Someone is trying to get through the door. They don't have a key—it sounds like they're trying to crash through.

My heart hammered, and I had to hope and pray to Fate that it was the Grimstone guys and not the Blackwood pack. I glanced over my shoulder to confirm with Ryker, but I could barely see him behind me.

Somehow I'd gotten at least seventy-five yards ahead of

him, which shouldn't have been possible, given how strong his wolf was. Knowing that waiting for him would probably take as much time as reaching Briar, I faced forward once more and kept pushing.

I could see the end of the neighborhood now, which meant I would be there soon. *I'm almost there, Briar. Just hold on.*

Terror seized my heart, and I pumped my arms harder. I gritted my teeth, needing to channel every ounce of effort into reaching her as quickly as I could.

Branches snapped, and I jerked my head to the right and saw a shadowed outline of a person in the woods.

I tensed, unsure whether the person was from Shae or Blackwood, but as long as they didn't try to prevent me from reaching my sister, I didn't give a damn.

The crack of splintering wood caught my attention, and Briar connected, *Three wolves just broke down the door.*

My gaze landed on a small one-story building at the end of the neighborhood. *I'm almost there. Fight them off if they try to harm you.*

Sounds of pain and suffering in the neighborhood grew deafening and merged with the memory of the deaths of my own pack.

The coldness in my chest iced over, and unshed tears burned my eyes. I blinked, clearing my vision, as Briar yelled, "Don't touch me!"

I rounded the corner of the small building, noticing it had only one exit, and bounded up the step and inside to find three muddy wolves surrounding a chained Briar, who lay on a bed.

And Bruce had tried to make it sound as if she wasn't a prisoner.

If he'd been with me now, I'd have been very tempted to rip his throat out.

Briar lifted her head, and her bloodshot eyes widened. "Ember, save yourself!"

All three wolves turned in my direction—they were the Grimstone pack.

I let out a shaky breath. "They're our fri–er–allies. You don't need to be alarmed." Even in crisis, I couldn't allow myself to call them more than they ever needed to be. Briar was the one person I could trust.

Gage whimpered and pointed his nose at one thick metal handcuff that bound Briar to the bed.

Her hair was stringy and greasy like she hadn't washed since she'd gotten here. Her arms were stretched over her head but with enough give in the chain for her to move around slightly.

We needed to get those cuffs off. I examined the metal links that each was attached to. The headboard would be too awkward to carry with her hands bound to it like that. For the first time, reality hit me. We might not make it out alive. "I need the key or an axe or something."

"Bobby pin." Briar pointed where the bed rested against the wall. "I dropped a bobby pin down there when I was trying to get it out of my hair the other day."

How the hell had she managed to get a bobby pin? But that was another question for another time. I pushed past Gage and Kendric and lowered myself to the gray vinyl floor.

Of course it had fallen against the wall near her head, meaning I had to crawl under the entire bed to reach it.

Rushed footsteps drew closer, along with the growls, snarls, and whimpers. The enemy was near, and I still didn't have Briar free.

I inched forward on my stomach until I snagged the tiny bit of cold metal between my fingertips. As soon as I began crawling out, Briar started screaming bloody murder.

Hands grabbed both my ankles and yanked me from under the bed. As soon as I emerged from underneath, I was flipped over to find a very angry and sexy Ryker glaring down at me.

I forgot how to breathe.

"You better not run off from me like that *ever* again," he snapped, the gold in his eyes not hidden by the sheen.

Before I could respond, he reached down and snatched the bobby pin from me and moved to my sister.

"Don't come near me," she whimpered.

"He's on our side," I rasped, climbing back to my feet.

Briar's jaw dropped. "But he's the Grimstone alpha."

"Who's going to get you out of these cuffs, and my pack is going to make sure that both you and your sister make it to safety." Ryker stretched out the bobby pin and got to work.

Briar scooted away, and I reached out to take the bobby pin from him, but my hands were shaking too hard. There was no way I'd be able to get her unlocked. There was only one option. "Trust him. We need to get you out of here."

"Okay." Briar bit her bottom lip and closed her eyes, allowing Ryker to get close to her without reacting.

I hurried to the door and peeked out to see what sort of hell we'd have to get through to escape. The fight was still going, and the stench of blood and that strange sensation from earlier both hung heavy in the air.

A wolf darted out of the tree line, and something like a shadowy outline ran after it, moving just as quickly. The shadow figure grabbed the wolf by the neck and lifted it high. The wolf snarled, snapping at the air, searching for the enemy as if he couldn't find it, and then the shadow figure's head lowered, and suddenly, the wolf's throat was ripped out.

Blood poured from the wolf's neck, and I gasped. What sort of magic were the Blackwoods using?

The shadow figure's head snapped up, and though I couldn't see its face or where it was looking, I didn't have to. The hair on the nape of my neck rose, and my wolf surged forward.

"We have enemies incoming," I muttered just as the shadow figure blurred toward me.

The three wolves hurried to my side, but the shadow was on me, a huge version of the iridescent sheen I'd noticed covering Ryker's eyes at times. It struck a hand at my shoulder, and I pivoted back so that the hand caught only air.

The three Grimstone wolves materialized beside me, and the shadow figure kicked out its right leg, nailing Xander in the face. Xander's head snapped back, and he whimpered as the shadow lifted Kendric by the neck.

Kendric snarled, his eyes rolling like crazy, searching for his attacker.

Realization pressed in.

No one else could see it!

The attacker lowered its head, and I knew what would happen next if I didn't act.

I kicked the shadow in its knee.

It crumpled and landed on top of Kendric. Kendric thrashed, trying to get free, but the shadow had already begun climbing on top of him. I reached down and grabbed the back of its neck, causing the shadow to swipe at my hands, its claws digging into my skin.

"Ember!" Briar exclaimed as I shoved the shadow into the wall, away from the wolves.

"Get out of here," I commanded. No one else seemed to

be able to see this thing, and I didn't want anyone else to get hurt. The Blackwoods had done enough.

My blood dripped to the floor, but I didn't give a shit.

I heard a click, and out of the corner of my eye, I saw Briar bound off the bed toward me. Her arms wrapped around me in a big hug, her back to the shadow. Clearly, she also couldn't see it.

A silver glint appeared at the shadow's side.

It had a knife.

"Get out of here now." I tried to shove Briar off, but she was latched on to me.

The shadow swung at her back, right where her heart would be.

"No," I shouted as I tried to move Briar aside.

I couldn't do it fast enough.

Then Ryker appeared in front of us...and the knife stabbed him in my sister's place.

My heart broke worse than ever before, and a scream rang out around us as Ryker dropped to the floor. Kendric, Gage, and Xander ran to their alpha's side. They growled and searched for the enemy...the very one who was now stepping around them, its attention on me.

The shadow laughed malevolently like it knew we were all going to die.

Fear strangled me, but I lifted my chin. If Ryker had sacrificed himself for me, then I wouldn't let his death be for nothing.

The strange, jolting power rushed through me, and I jumped to my feet.

I would protect my sister and take this shadow down for hurting my people and Ryker, even if I died trying.

ABOUT THE AUTHOR

Jen L. Grey is a *USA Today* Bestselling Author who writes Paranormal Romance, Urban Fantasy, and Fantasy genres.

Jen lives in Tennessee with her husband, two daughters, and two miniature Australian Shepherds. Before she began writing, she was an avid reader and enjoyed being involved in the indie community. Her love for books eventually led her to writing. For more information, please visit her website and sign up for her newsletter.

Check out her future projects and book signing events at her website.

www.jenlgrey.com

ALSO BY JEN L. GREY

Of Fae and Wolf Trilogy

Bonded to the Fallen Shadow King

Rejected Fate Trilogy

Betrayed Mate

Fated To Darkness

The King of Frost and Shadows

The Court of Thorns and Wings

The Kingdom of Flames and Ash

The Forbidden Mate Trilogy

Wolf Mate

Wolf Bitten

Wolf Touched

Standalone Romantasy

Of Shadows and Fae

Twisted Fate Trilogy

Destined Mate

Eclipsed Heart

Chosen Destiny

The Marked Dragon Prince Trilogy

Ruthless Mate

Marked Dragon

Hidden Fate

Shadow City: Silver Wolf Trilogy

Broken Mate

Rising Darkness

Silver Moon

Shadow City: Royal Vampire Trilogy

Cursed Mate

Shadow Bitten

Demon Blood

Shadow City: Demon Wolf Trilogy

Ruined Mate

Shattered Curse

Fated Souls

Shadow City: Dark Angel Trilogy

Fallen Mate

Demon Marked

Dark Prince

Fatal Secrets

Shadow City: Silver Mate

Shattered Wolf

Fated Hearts

Ruthless Moon

The Wolf Born Trilogy

Hidden Mate

Blood Secrets

Awakened Magic

The Hidden King Trilogy

Dragon Mate

Dragon Heir

Dragon Queen

The Marked Wolf Trilogy

Moon Kissed

Chosen Wolf

Broken Curse

Wolf Moon Academy Trilogy

Shadow Mate

Blood Legacy

Rising Fate

The Royal Heir Trilogy

Wolves' Queen

Wolf Unleashed

Wolf's Claim

Bloodshed Academy Trilogy

Year One

Year Two

Year Three

The Half-Breed Prison Duology (Same World As Bloodshed Academy)

Hunted

Cursed

The Artifact Reaper Series

Reaper: The Beginning

Reaper of Earth

Reaper of Wings

Reaper of Flames

Reaper of Water

Stones of Amaria (Shared World)

Kingdom of Storms

Kingdom of Shadows

Kingdom of Ruins

Kingdom of Fire

The Pearson Prophecy

Dawning Ascent

Enlightened Ascent

Reigning Ascent

Stand Alones

Printed in Great Britain
by Amazon